DANCING

INTO

DESTINY

DANCING

INTO

DESTINY

By

Toni Marie Weber

Toni Marie Weber

Dedication

To Art, my wonderful husband and the love of my life.

Thank you for the precious love that you gave to me and for the honor of being your wife.

The lovely memories that we made together will live in my heart until our joyous reunion on the other side.

Acknowledgments

Thanks to my writing group: Nancy, Sean, Teresa, and Julie for the help in fine tuning the writing, always with a gentle hand. But, most importantly, for your encouragement, support and friendship. Without you guys this wouldn't have happened. I only hope that I can be as much of a help to all of you with the wonderful books that you are writing.

Thanks to my dear friends who read the manuscript and offered support and editing suggestions: Marie, Bobbi, Diane, Linda, Nancy.

My gratitude to Dan Lowe, for taking the time to critique this work at the TAZ Writer's Workshop and for the support and encouragement that he offered.

Finally a huge thank you to my sweet friend, Nancy. It is so great that we can embark on this writing journey together. I can't wait to see your completed book!

Cover Credit

Painting "Dancing into Destiny" by Toni Weber.

Photoshop Magic by Nancy Seman. You are amazing!

Chapter 1

Lying there, tears filling the corner of his bright blue eyes.

"I'm greedy," he said. "Don't worry about me, I've done everything that I wanted to do, lived my life to the fullest. But, I'm greedy. I just want more time with you. More time to touch your hair, kiss your lips, time."

The room had gone silent. The constant beeping of the heart monitors gone. Unplugged. The tubes pulled. The silence deafening. Only an hour ago, the room filled with the whirring of machines, the constant in and out of nurses and doctors. Now, nothing.

Only the silent, darkening room.

I sat beside him, as was my habit each moment of every day. Holding his hand, looking into his eyes. Those eyes, ever sparkling with life, with love. Now filled with sadness, resignation. All hope dissipated.

I began to weep, no words would come, my heart breaking within me. So much that I longed to tell him, but the lump in my throat caught them and pushed them back deep into my heart.

"You must find someone else," Jake continued, the tears flowing freely now. Ever gallant, strong. Ever thinking of me. In his effort to set me free, he remarked again, "You are too sweet a woman to live alone. I want you to be happy again, to love again."

The selflessness of those words broke down the dam and the tears streamed from my body, heaving with the pain of knowing I was losing him, no denying that now.

The absence of machines, of doctors all pointing to the fact that the end was near. Abandonment and hopelessness filled the shadowy room and threatened to crush us.

"No," I managed to whisper, "No one could ever replace you. You are the love of my life. The only person whom I have felt truly loved me. My heart belongs to you forever."

The loud clanging of the wheel chair entering the room startled me. I jumped in my chair. That is it then, I thought, nothing more to be done, just wait.

The hospice workers were on the front porch when we arrived home. How did they get there so fast? It was their show now, the end of life crew. How do they do it day after day, watching as life slips away from each person they serve?

They worked efficiently connecting equipment, delivering morphine. I watched as they wrapped the oxygen tubing around Jake's ears and over to his nose.

This weak, thin, shell of a man. A man once so full of the zest for life, fearless. He was courageous as he jumped from the plane on his first skydiving experience, though he admitted that standing in the open door gave him pause. He tackled the three rivers on water skies and snorkeled in the Caribbean. There was nothing that he would shrink back from. His strength and confidence filled a room as soon as he entered.

To see him lying there, broken, tore my heart out. Even still, when he looked at me, the twinkle remained, the boyish grin, the wink that betrayed the desire that lingered even then. The thought of saying good bye to this man was too much to bear. His presence didn't just fill a room, no, it filled my heart and soul and reached into my very being. I feared that his absence would mean the emptiness of life itself. I noticed the quickening of my heart beat and realized I was holding my breath.

The nurse informed me that we would receive the prescriptions through the Hospice program now. They will deliver any time day or night. She encouraged me to call at any time, someone is always at the center to answer any questions or be of service. She was gentle and kind, rubbing Jake's shoulder as she instructed us.

I listened to her intently, trying to retain everything she was saying, but it was a struggle. I could feel the panic rising within me. How can I take care of him, I'm not a nurse. What if something happens?

I wanted them to leave, but I was afraid to be alone with Jake, his sole protector.

As the nurse opened the door to leave she turned around and our eyes met, she gave me a sad smile. "It will be alright," she said quietly, but I knew it wouldn't.

Everything was happening too fast.

Chapter 2

I n the privacy of our home, Jake lay on the sofa. I cradled his head in my lap, my thoughts going to the first time we met. I could see it as clearly as if it were yesterday.

It was a crisp September day in Pittsburgh. The advertising agency had acquired the fundraising contract for the fire department. All of the staff were invited to bring their children to the fire station to film the public service commercial. The trucks had been washed and polished and their bright red paint gleamed in the sunlight. The fire fighters stood beside the trucks in their full gear of black and yellow over hauls and rubber boots. They had unraveled one of the fire hoses so the boys could see just how large they were.

We were all gathered on the sidewalk that Saturday awaiting our turn to climb aboard the fire engine. The children giggled, hardly able to contain their excitement. Something, someone caught my eye. A man stood beside the truck. Something about him called to me. His hair looked like spun gold beneath the bright light of the sun. His little boy sat upon his strong, broad shoulders giggling. His muscles rippled as he lifted his son off of his shoulders and on to the seat of the fire truck. It was a scene from a Norman Rockwell painting. The hominess and love shining through. A small town image in the center of the city. His tight black jeans and muscle builder t shirt clung to his slim 6'4" figure. A pair of black shiny cowboy boots completed the picture, making him appear even taller.

Oh, he didn't notice me standing behind the other parents with my little boy, but he took my breath away causing my heart to beat faster. Who was that man? He reached into the truck and showed his son all of the controls and what they were for, the boy's smile broad and bright. That was the first moment I saw him. And it is seared in my memory and will no doubt remain there forever.

I sidled up to Sarah, one of the other secretaries, and whispered, "Who is that man there, the tall one at the fire truck? I have never seen him before."

"Oh, that's Jake Thompson, the new advertising executive. He just arrived from Colorado. Isn't he divine?"

I stole another look, Jake huh? Hmmmm.

For the rest of the weekend my thoughts would drift back to Jake and the way he looked in those tight jeans. The gentle way that he spoke to his son and patiently explained the buttons and controls only enhanced his appeal. The love that they had for each other shone through both of their faces. It was easy to see that he was a hero in his son's eyes. I wondered if he was married, attached?

Chapter 3

The weekly pitch meetings were held on Monday mornings. I grabbed a cup of coffee from the kitchen and made my way into the conference room. I found a seat at the table and rummaged through my purse for my reading glasses. When I looked up, Jake was sitting across from me. As soon as our eyes met, a friendly smile graced his face.

"Oh, hello, my name is Tina," I stammered stretching out my hand to shake his.

"I'm Jake." His hand lingered with mine just a little too long.

I was caught off guard but managed to stutter out, "Pleasure to meet you."

"The pleasure is mine I assure you." His eyes were as blue and deep as the ocean and I needed to look away for the fear that he would see right through to my soul.

Mike Harrison was the president of the firm. He stood at the head of the conference table and pointed toward Jake. "This is Jake, everyone. Please give him a warm welcome. Jake is going to be heading up the public relations for the fire department. He's going to need someone to help him with the campaign. It's a great cause and we want to make sure to help them raise as much money as possible. Glancing at me, he said, "Tina, clear your projects. I want you to work closely with Jake as his personal assistant. I have no doubt that with the two of you on the job it will be a most successful campaign."

I had worked with Jim Sarver, one of the Vice Presidents of the firm, on the library fundraising project last fall. We were able to secure enough money to add a new wing to the library as well as secure an additional 10,000 books for the collection. It seemed that Jim must have given a good report of my work to Mike. The fire department campaign would be a good opportunity for me to prove myself once again.

Mike went on to discuss a few more issues, but I didn't hear a thing. All I could think of was that I would be working side by side with Jake every day. The thought of spending each day by his side filled me with excitement, and dread.

When the meeting adjourned Jake came over to my side of the table.

"Hey Tina, we should get started right away. How about you meet me in my office in an hour? We will have to get you settled in the office next to mine."

"Sure, I'll just get my things together and see you in an hour."

Sarah caught up with me in the hall. "You're so lucky to be working with Jake. I'm so jealous." She whispered squeezing my arm.

"Hope you're right, just wondering what he will be like as a boss."

"Well, he seems really nice, if all else fails, at least he's nice to look at. Nothing wrong with having a little eye candy in your life each day." Sarah said winking and walked away laughing.

Sarah was in her early forties but looked thirty, thanks to her straight red hair and the freckles that covered her nose and face. She was five foot nothing and thin, a little wisp of a thing. Sarah had been at the agency five years longer than I. When I arrived on board she helped to show me the ropes, who to stay away from and who I could trust. She had become a close friend, and the one I trusted the most. Many a weekend we would leave our husbands to watch the children for the day while we took in lunch or a movie.

Jake met me at the door to my office and took the stacks of files out of my hands and placed them on the desk. Then he helped me move the desk in front of the window. That was unheard of. The other bosses expected their secretaries to do everything for them, not the other way around. So casual and unassuming, I liked him already.

"Tina, I like my assistants to have a say in how the campaign is run. You're not just someone to type up my letters or submit my bills. We're going to be a team. I want you to feel free to tell me your thoughts and ideas about the fundraising. How about you take some time to get settled in to your office and then we grab a quick lunch and get to know each other a little bit?"

I had been working here for ten years and this was the first time that I was being asked my opinion. It was so exciting. So many times I had ideas, but, just being a secretary, had to keep them to myself. Secretly I wanted to become an ad executive myself but didn't feel they would consider me seriously, maybe things would change now. It sure would be great to have my own group of clients and head up a team.

As we entered Tom's Diner, Jake asked for the corner booth and ordered two cups of coffee. The booth could hardly contain his long legs. As they slightly brushed against mine, a spark of electricity shot up my thighs. I felt flushed with desire and wondered if he felt it too. If he noticed the color rising in my cheeks.

"Call me crazy," Jake began, "But for some reason I don't believe that you're the run of the mill secretary. Tell me, what college did you go to and what was your major?"

"Oh," I stammered. "Wow. I, um, I went to the University of Pittsburgh in the evenings and weekends. I majored in writing and studio arts. Most of the writing was in journalism, graduated a few months ago."

"Does Mike know that you completed the degree? I just can't imagine that he wouldn't hire you on as an ad executive now that you have the sheepskin. Why don't we see about getting you the hands on experience? Maybe it will open some doors for you, if that's what you want."

"Are you kidding? That would be a dream come true! I would certainly appreciate it. Not too many women move up this corporate ladder and I could sure use the help. Thanks."

The rest of the lunch was filled with small talk. Jake had a wife, Mindy, and one son, Charlie. Charlie was in the fourth grade. He was adjusting well to the move and the new school. They bought a house south of the city when they arrived here from Denver, Colorado.

We laughed at the fact that I also lived south of the city and had a son, Sam, in fourth grade. Small world, the boys were actually in the same school and same class. What were the odds? I told him that I was married and my husband, John, was unemployed at the time and taking night classes in heating and air conditioning. It seemed like a good idea to get the two boys together for an outing, something that we were going to work on.

Time passed quickly and the conversation flowed effortlessly as if we were already old friends. Too soon, it was time to go back to the office. My heart soared, could this really be the break that I was waiting for? John and I could sure use the extra money that a promotion would bring. Even if he didn't work steady, the increase in my salary would make it easier to pay the bills and maybe do some fun things as well. The hopefulness I felt put a spring in my step.

Most days, Jake and I could be seen sitting side by side with Jake going over the numbers and plans for advertising the fundraising events. Sometimes his leg would rest upon mine. If he realized it, he never let on, and never moved it. The heat of his touch seared against my flesh as I struggled to concentrate. It was hard to fight the enormous attraction that I felt for this man.

Chapter 4

John was a sheet metal worker before we got married. He had a good salary, but, at 33 years old, he felt that he was too old to continue to work out in the ever changing Pittsburgh weather. He left the union a month before our wedding. During the following nine years he had several jobs from caretaker to insurance salesman. Each time he had a disagreement with a co-worker or was over looked for a promotion, he left the position. This kept us living from paycheck to paycheck and the ensuing financial stress was putting extreme pressure on us. He decided to become a stationary engineer. To that end he started attending tech school for heating and air conditioning in the evenings. I had hoped that going to school would set him on a more positive course. But things had gotten more strained between us. It seemed that the slightest irritation would send him into a rage. More than once a bowl of cereal went flying through the air smashing against the wall. The glass shattering and spraying across the room while the cream of wheat adhered to the wall turning to cement in short order.

At the first sound of his dad's raised voice, Sam would run for cover in his room and close his door. In my first marriage, I learned not to fight back. With John I measured my words carefully trying to gage what might be the cause of the next emotional explosion and how to avoid it. When John did erupt, I would get out of the way and then quietly clean up the mess. Later we never talked about the incident. Just pretended it didn't happen.

Sam never invited his friends over to play at our house.

It soon got easier to just avoid being with John altogether. My son, Sam, had a friend, Matt, who lived two houses away. Sam would go to Matt's house after school and stay there until I returned from work. Matt's mom, Rose, was very kind and opened her home to Sam. She could hear the yelling resonating from our house and was happy to give Sam a safe haven until I returned home each evening. The boys loved having the time to play together and I was grateful to know that Sam was in good hands.

In order to avoid seeing John, I began staying later at work. I carefully timed it so that I would arrive home shortly after John left for school. He wouldn't get back home until eleven, and I would make sure I was asleep in bed by then. In the morning I would wake up early to get Sam off to school and leave for work before John was out of bed.

It didn't take very long for Jake to notice that I was delaying going home. After only one week of working overtime, I noticed that Jake's light was still on in his office after 5:00. The rest of our co-workers had long since gone home.

I was busy typing some letters when I felt Jake's presence enter the room. I heard the door click shut behind him. My breath caught as I looked in his face and saw the same desire on it that I felt in my body.

Without a single word, Jake walked towards me, stepped behind me and leaned against the window sill.

"What's going on Tina?" he asked.

"Just have some letters that I need to get out." I said glancing at him and then quickly looking away. My eyes were directly across from his crotch. Yikes, don't look up, don't look up. Did he see that?

Jake seemed to read my mind. Silently he took my hand and lifted me out of the chair. Then he sat down on the chair himself and pulled me down on to his lap. I could feel his rising desire beneath me and felt the breath catch in my throat.

He tenderly lifted my face to his. His lips were soft and moist. He slightly opened them and I opened my lips in response. His tongue slipped in exploring, sensual. The kiss seemed to go on forever, when I came to my senses I gently pulled away.

What am I doing? I panicked. We are both married. This isn't who I am.

But his arms encircled me and made me feel safe. I wanted to stay in those arms forever.

"We can't do this." I whispered.

"I know, I'm sorry, it is just that it has been on my mind for so long. Sorry, it won't happen again. I promise."

We heard a click and the door opened. It was the night maid. She looked at the two of us and quickly looked away and closed the door.

"We had better get out of here." Jake said. "Before we do something we'll regret. It's dark, I'll walk you to your car."

Jake helped me on with my coat. We walked silently down the hall, not looking at each other. The sexual tension between us palpable. We entered the elevator and descended to the garage, still silent. Would we be able to work together, keep our emotions in check now that they were out?

Jake walked me to my car and helped me open the door. He glanced around the garage and noticing no one around, pulled me close to him once more. His desire stronger than the risk.

"It won't happen again, but I need one last kiss." He said, his hot breath danced upon my ear, igniting my passion again.

His arms encircled me. I was pushed up against my car and could feel him growing hard against me. My breath was ragged, heart racing. It took all of my will to finally pull away and enter my car.

Riding home a great sadness enveloped me. Why did I have to be stuck in a loveless marriage when this wonderful man was right there in front of me? Still right was right. Right?

Jake walked sadly to his car. What was he doing? Didn't he have a wife at home who depended on him? And his son, Charlie, he could never do anything to hurt him. He loved that boy more than words could say.

Chapter 5

The last year had taken a toll on Jake's marriage. His wife, Mindy, was a sales person. She did okay, but not well enough to support herself.

It was last winter that it happened. They were living in Colorado then. Sure, he worked long hours, but it was for them. Somehow Mindy couldn't understand that the long hours were necessary if they wanted to get ahead, have a comfortable life. The advertising business was competitive, if you didn't keep up you would be left behind.

Bored, alone and too much time on her hands, Mindy needed an escape. The financial insecurities over the winter added to the strain on their marriage. She concocted a believable story for a week long sales conference in Aspen. Drawn into her web without questioning, Jake arranged for Charlie's after school care.

After the conference, Mindy grew more distant from him. They hardly spoke and more often than not, when he returned home at night, he would find Charlie sitting with the babysitter watching television. She never explained where she was, only said it was work.

Maybe in his heart he knew something was wrong, but he didn't ask questions, didn't want to know the answers. The more uncertain he felt, the harder he threw himself into his work. The head of the firm noticed his dedication. Jake had increased the clientele and had glowing reports from them. They loved his ad ideas and sales were up. He was called into the office and given a promotion. Finally they could buy the home they dreamed about. Everything would be better now, he was sure of it. He could work less hours, maybe they could take a long needed vacation together.

It was the middle of the day. Jake rushed home to tell Mindy the good news. He pulled into the drive. So excited. He entered the apartment yelling her name, "Mindy, Mindy."

It was strangely quiet, he walked back to the bedroom. Through the door he could hear Mindy's familiar moaning. The sound of the door opening startled her boss, Alex. He jumped out of bed and retreated to the far back wall. Afraid of Jake's reaction.

But Jake just stood there, broken hearted. He felt like he was in a cheap movie, just a cliché. Her lover grabbed his clothes and ran from the room giving Jake a wide berth. Jake and Mindy just looked at each other. Is this how it would end, just as things were turning around?

He didn't say a word and she didn't offer an explanation. Silence. Deafening silence filled the room.

The next day Mindy didn't go to work, Jake called off. They got their son off to school, put on some coffee and sat at the dining table.

"So, are you in love with him?" Jake asked.

Mindy couldn't look at him, but stared down at the floor. Tears of shame filling her eyes.

"Look I know I haven't been around much. But all the long hours have paid off, I just got a huge promotion, we can buy that house we always wanted. That's why I came home early, to tell you. If you still want to be married to me, we can work through this. It will be hard, but we can do it if we try. What do you think?"

Mindy continued to look at the floor. "Could you really forgive me?"

"I'm not saying it won't be hard. Trust broken takes a long time to build again. Maybe what we need is a fresh start. I can ask for a transfer to Pittsburgh. That way I still get the promotion. Maybe a new city, new friends, will help. A fresh start, try to put this all behind us. I'm willing to try if you are."

The transfer was approved a few months ago, that is when he started working for Mike. Mindy had found a new sales job in Pittsburgh. Their relationship was still strained. Hard as he tried, the betrayal was always before him, could he really trust her.

Now this.

So, he must not have forgiven her after all. How else could he explain this attraction to Tina? His reckless actions tonight. Seeing her unhappiness had reminded him of his own. Didn't they deserve to be happy?

He arrived home, dropped his keys in the tray and headed for the shower. Maybe the hot steam would clear his mind, make some sense of this, knock some sense into him, and relieve his heavy heart.

He stood in the shower. Thoughts of Tina filled his mind. He could still taste her sweet lips, feel her body against his, smell her perfume.

Chapter 6

I could hardly keep my mind on the road as I headed home. John had already left for school. I picked Sam up at Matt's house. He sat at the dining table doing his homework as I prepared dinner.

The memory of Jake's kiss lingered on my lips. I could still smell his after shave and feel the tenderness of his warm embrace. I tried to put it out of my mind as I chopped vegetables and poured milk. I had lost my appetite but sat with Sam as he ate. Then I got Sam into bed.

As soon as I thought Sam was asleep I poured myself a glass of wine, put on some slow jazz, started a bubble bath and tried to make sense of everything that happened. What was I going to do tomorrow? I needed this job. Jake promised that it wouldn't happen again. Somehow that thought just made me sad.

I arrived at work the next day, grabbed a cup of coffee and went to my office. A moment later the intercom buzzed.

"Tina, can you come in here please?" It was Jake.

"Sure."

Not sure what to expect, I slowly walked next door.

"Close the door behind you please."

I did just that, my heart pounding. Was I fired?

"Look, things got carried away last night. I'm sorry, can you forgive me? It won't happen again, I promise. Let's just try to work together, we make a pretty great team, don't you think?"

"Yes, yes. I'm sorry too. Thank you."

"Okay, great, just get your coffee then and come back when you're ready."

With that we resumed our business relationship and didn't speak of it again. Trouble was, I kept thinking of it. Jake's face haunted me when I was away from the office. I longed for his tender touch and the sweet taste of his lips.

Chapter 7

John and I hardly saw each other during the week and the weekends were filled with stress. Sam started spending more time at Matt's house. Left at home alone with John, I would busy myself cleaning the house or cooking dinner, not knowing when John's rage would flare up. When it did, I quietly cleaned up the mess. Was this the way it would always be?

I felt trapped.

Then everything changed.

It was July 3 and I was getting ready to go grocery shopping. Normally I would cut coupons and check the fliers for all three grocery stores nearby. Since money was tight, we would go from one shop to the other buying the sale items and submitting the weekly coupons. That morning I was feeling down and not up to the arduous task.

The day before we had attended a reunion of the employees of a Christian coffeehouse where I had worked. Seeing everyone else doing so well and so "holy" had made me feel bad about my life, the direction it had taken and the struggles it entailed.

"I don't feel like cutting the coupons today and going to all the shops. Let's just go to one store and get what we need. Okay?" I said as I plopped into the chair by the window.

"Why, what's wrong?" John asked coming towards me.

"Nothing, I just don't feel like doing all that today."

Maybe the disappointment or the vague feeling of depression showed on my face because something certainly enraged John.

He ran over to me and began hitting me, I kicked my legs out to keep him away. Then I jumped up and grabbed my purse. John picked up a large potted plant and threw it at me, the dirt flying all over the floor. That was the last straw. I picked up the heavy pot and threw it at him, just missing his head.

"I can throw things too," I yelled.

He looked at me in disbelief. His mouth agape with surprise. For nine years I had kept quiet when he would demonstrate his rage. It was the first time I stood up for myself. He couldn't compute that this woman who had quietly accepted the abuse time after time had suddenly set her own anger free. He didn't know how to handle it and couldn't say a word.

I grabbed my son's hand and my purse and we ran down the steps and out of the house. As I looked back, John had recovered from his stupor and was picking up a coffee can filled with bolts and heaved it at us. We were moving too fast and the can missed us and hit his truck, the side window shattered, exploding all over the sidewalk. The coffee can landed on the cement and preceded to chase us down the hill.

John had a way of always making himself the victim. Some unknown people always at fault for keeping him down. It was clear that with my actions today, I had now become the enemy, there was no turning back. No way to redeem myself now.

Sam and I ran to the local church for refuge. The secretary, Ginny, agreed to drive me to my parent's house. Ginny drove down my street and Rose, came running out to tell me that John had left. Ginny and Sam stayed in the car with the motor running like a getaway car. Rose and I grabbed some garbage bags and ran into the house to pack Sam's things and some of my clothes. We worked feverishly worried that John would return home at any moment. Rose said that she would pick Sam up after school the next day. Ginny drove us to my parent's home.

We knocked on the door.

"Hi, Tina! We didn't expect you. Come on in. I'll put on some coffee." my mom beamed.

As soon as her kind words hit my ears, the dam broke and the tears gushed forth. My dad came over and put his arms around me. I couldn't say anything as I sobbed.

"What's wrong? What has happened?" They asked concerned and baffled.

"Daddy hit mommy." Sam offered. A fact that I wanted to hide from them. Why was I still protecting him? "We had to run to the church, Miss Ginny drove us here. Daddy threw something at us and it was rolling down the street behind us." Sam said excitedly.

They both turned to look at me.

"Things have been bad between us for a long time. I thought that going to school would be a good thing. That he would finally be happier, but it has only gotten worse. He is always angry and tonight was the last straw."

I struggled to keep my emotions in check, my lower lip quivering, as I told them about the flying dishes and flower pots. They were shocked, for nine years I had hidden it all from them. Now I told them everything at the same time assuring Sam that we would be okay, hiding the panic I felt deep inside. Compassion filled their eyes as they listened to my sad tale.

They stared at me in disbelief, eyes wide. "Oh, my gosh! We had no idea! Why didn't you tell us this was going on?" Mom asked. "I'm so sorry, you must have felt so alone through all of this." She said hugging me.

"You and Sam can stay here tonight, in fact, stay here as long as you need to." Dad said putting his arm around me and pulling Sam to his side.

The familiar surroundings of my childhood home felt like a sanctuary from the harsh realities of life. Their comforting words and embraces encircled Sam and I and immersed us in liquid love.

As I lay alone in my old bedroom, the one I shared with my older sister growing up, I reviewed all that happened that day. John knew that I would never stand for him hitting Sam or I. Could it be that he wanted out of the marriage but was unable to ask for a divorce. Was this his way of making it my decision to leave?

He knew my past. At 20 years old, I had been married for 6 months. It was a turbulent courtship that led to an abusive marriage. One that I fled from. I vowed that it would never happen to me again.

It was a hot September night in the city. My friend Rhonda and I had just moved into an apartment together. We were two young birds leaving the nest and the safety and protection of our families for the first time. The Christian Coffeehouse with its free concerts lured us into the inner city like a moth to a flame. We were shocked to see homeless inhabitants huddled in doorways mostly invisible to the passersby.

The scene changed dramatically around the corner where the acoustic guitar and harmonious voices echoed through the air and young people filled the coffeehouse and overflowed into the street. Standing room only.

We shuffled our way to the door and stood on tip toes to get a glance of the handsome young singer strumming and vocalizing. A quick glance was all we got as we were nudged back out the door to join the overflow. Four fellows spied us from across the street and made their way to our side.

Rhonda and I just looked at each other.

Joey spoke up first, "So you young ladies must be new here, don't remember seeing you before. Allow me to introduce myself, Joey, Moses for short." He gave us a quick grin that sported a chipped front tooth. When he moved his head, his afro seemed to move in the other direction.

"This here is Frank, my brother," he pointed to a tall fellow beside him with curly black hair and a quick grin as well. Frank's grin was minus the chip and broad and bright.

Next on the agenda was a short, blonde haired man sporting a blazer with patches on the sleeves and a pipe, although it was not clear whether there was any tobacco in the pipe. "This is Danny, we call him professor."

21

The last member of the crew stepped closer to Moses. Impatient at not being introduced sooner. He was around 5' 7" with long sandy colored hair and hazel eyes, "I'm Glenn," he offered.

We spent the evening joking and laughing together. Glenn asked if Rhonda and I would like to go to Ohio Pyle the next morning. Ohio Pyle is a park in southern Pennsylvania with raging rapids and hiking trails. It was a two hour drive so we decided he could stay at our apartment in order to get an early start. We gave him a blanket and pillow for the couch while Rhonda and I retreated to our bedroom and locked the door behind us.

When the alarm went off, Rhonda decided not to go along, so Glenn and I headed off together. We got there before sunrise. In the pitch blackness of the park, stars crowded the sky. It was a meteor shower and the shooting stars raced from one side of the sky to the other. We watched for a while and then fell off to sleep awaiting the sunrise.

It was a pleasant day as we hiked in the woods. We enjoyed the peanut butter and jelly sandwiches that I had packed as we sat on a large boulder that shot out over the falls. We headed for home around one o'clock.

We arrived back at my apartment around 3:00 in the afternoon. Rhonda was still at work. Glenn decided to call the coffeehouse to tell them he wouldn't be in to work that day. As he spoke to his boss it was clear that Terry wasn't happy with Glenn, apparently he had been absent from work before. Glenn was getting agitated and harsh words were spoken.

He hung up the phone and I asked if everything was okay. Without a word, Glenn pushed me down on the sofa. He grabbed my arm and lifted it over my head. I struggled, confused at what was happening. He held me down with his body and grabbed my other arm and put it over my head as well. Now he was able to hold both of my arms down with one of his hands. With his weight on top of my legs, he proceeded to pull my clothes off. I begged him to stop, I had never been with a man before and I was afraid. The more that I begged and cried the more determined he became. He started to laugh at me, mocking my pleas. As he entered me, the pain was intense. I couldn't believe what was happening, and didn't understand how everything had changed in only a few moments. When he was done, he got up and left the apartment without a word, leaving me lying there in disbelief and horror.

I didn't go to school the next week. In fact, I never returned to the Art Institute at all.

That was how it started. Started, what was I thinking? Hard to believe that wasn't where it ended. Of course John didn't know this part. No one did.

All that John knew was that I was married before and lived in Alaska. I didn't share anything else with him until the night I stopped breathing.

It's funny how the absence of someone breathing beside you can wake you up just as surely as a scream. John woke up and shook me, "Tina, wake up. Tina!" When I didn't respond, he shook me again, harder. Still no response, he slapped me. I awoke with a start. In my dream I was taking a shower and Glenn came into the room and started stabbing me. "I don't understand, why would you have such a dream?" He asked. It was then that I told John a little about what happened in Alaska isolated from my family and friends. The full story wouldn't come out for years to come.

Glenn and I had gotten married in Denver in July 1974, nine months after we met. Right after we got married we moved from Denver to Fairbanks. He was going to work on the pipeline. Instead he had gotten a job at a local warehouse. We had been in Fairbanks a couple of months when Glenn lost his job. He became angry and agitated at everything. I had a job making donuts at the Safeway supermarket. Looking back on it now, I can see that it was the same reaction he had that first day that we were together.

It was on a snowy Saturday in October. He came in to the apartment and started yelling at me to pack. He threw the suitcase down and started throwing my clothes around. It wasn't clear why he was doing this but it made me mad. I screamed "No!" to him. With that he reached out and grabbed me around the throat. He lifted me off the ground, my legs dangling in the air as he held me tightly around the neck and squeezed. His eyes looked like that of a mad man, open much too wide and filled with hate. A voice in my head told me to cough. But I didn't need to cough, I was stunned. The voice persisted in a more urgent tone now, cough! I

23

pretended to cough as best I could with him squeezing my wind pipe. At the sound of my cough, he looked surprised. His eyes went back to normal and he dropped me and ran from the apartment.

I had stayed in the marriage for a few more months until the violence escalated and I found myself face to face with a 44 caliber rifle, and the only way to insure my safety was to flee back to Pittsburgh. When I shared this part of the story with John, I told him that I would never tolerate abuse again, and especially not when a child was involved.

So, that brought up the question, why after years of throwing things and tantrums had he stepped over the line and struck me. Or was it inevitable that things would escalate? Feeling like a two time loser. I finally drifted off to sleep.

Chapter 8

The next morning Sam seemed fine, actually excited to be at grandma's house. She made him cereal with strawberries for breakfast, his favorite. We all drove Sam to school.

"Don't forget, Matt's mom is picking you up after school today. I'll pick you up at their house after I get off work."

"Okay, mom."

"Do you think you should wait a few days and think it over before getting a lawyer?" Mom asked.

"No, mom, this isn't an isolated incident. John and I have been having problems for years. Right now, I have the momentum to follow through. Last night I looked in the phone book and found a divorce lawyer close to my office. On my way to work, I'll stop and see him and get the paper work going. Can you drive me to my apartment? I want to see if John ever went back there and ask Louie to change the locks on the doors."

The downstairs neighbor told me that she never heard John come back. Mom and Dad went back to their place while I walked down six houses to the landlord's house. Louie answered the door. I told him what happened.

"John isn't working right now so he can't pay the rent, but, I would like to stay here. That would give Sam some stability during all of this. Is that okay with you?"

"Sure," Louie said, "I'll go up right now and change the locks. Any trouble, you know I'm right here for you. So sorry for your troubles, Tina. Please don't hesitate to call me."

The apartment already seemed more peaceful, just knowing that John would not be back. That was really all Sam and I wanted, peace and safety. I walked to Rose's house.

Rose was a short, ample Italian woman, who seemed to emote love from every pore. She had a genuine smile and smelled like cookies. No wonder Sam loved to come to her place. I barely knocked on the door when it opened and she beckoned me inside.

"How are you and Sam?" Rose said, grabbing my arm and leading me in.

"We're doing okay. I just spoke to my neighbor and John never came back so Sam and I are going to stay in our apartment. Sam doesn't know this yet. He will be so happy to know that we're still going to live close to you guys. Thanks for agreeing to pick him up today. I'll come get him right after work. You are a life saver!"

"No problem, Tina. Glad to help." Rose's arms embraced me in a warm bear hug. The kind that makes you feel safe.

The bus left me off a few blocks from the lawyer's office. After signing the divorce papers, I walked to work, got as far as the lobby and just couldn't face going upstairs. I walked to the bank of pay phones against the wall and called Sarah.

"Sarah, something has happened and I won't be able to make it to work this morning. Cover for me, will you? I'll fill you in later, promise. Can you please tell Jake I won't be in?"

I turned around to leave the building and saw Jake walking in the far door at the other end of the lobby. I quickly turned around ducking my head ever so slightly. Trying to be invisible.

Tears filled my eyes as I wondered how John and I got here, to this place. And what was I going to do now? How could I take care of this child alone? My heart was breaking. It was sad to witness the death of a marriage, even one that was filled with tension. Where were those two young people in love, filled with hopes and dreams on their wedding day so long ago? We were going to have a lot of kids and buy a house in the country. Now all of those dreams lay at my feet like shattered glass.

My heart hurt.

I felt like a failure.

My mind went back to the time that John and I met. It was January 1975. I had only returned from Alaska in December and was trying to get some direction in my life. Rhonda had moved to Missouri. Left without many friends, I joined the youth group at the First Presbyterian Church in downtown Pittsburgh. Sixty young adults headed off for a retreat in Ligonier, Pa. John and I were two of them.

John was a little bit older than the rest of us and worked for the sheet metal union. He stood 5' 9" and sported a handlebar mustache fashioned after Robert Redford's in the Jeremiah Johnson movie. His sandy brown hair and black cowboy hat accented his light blue eyes.

John had been engaged to Mary, one of the other girls in the group, but she had just broken up with him the week before. He seemed quiet and pensive. Throughout the weekend, I would notice him sitting alone.

At one point, we were seated at the dinner table together. He was easy to talk to and had a calm demeanor. When the weekend ended, we had made plans to go out for dinner.

Our relationship progressed quickly and by June we had decided to get married. John bought me a solitary diamond engagement ring. We set the date for Valentine's Day the following year, 1976. John had met my family a few times, but, I didn't want him with me when I told them about the engagement. I knew my parents wouldn't be happy – not that it had anything to do with him. No, it had everything to do with me, and the fact that I had just gotten home from a bad marriage six months ago. I insisted that I had to do this alone.

The sun was shining brightly that Wednesday in June. I took two buses and arrived at my family home at 5:00, in time for dinner. I peered into the kitchen before knocking and could see Mom cooking away while Dad sat at the dining room table. Some old Frank Sinatra song was playing on the stereo.

I knocked on the door. Mom turned around and saw me through the window, her look of surprise quickly changed to a smile. She opened the door and grabbed me in her arms for a tight hug. "Hi, what are you doing here in the middle of the week?" She asked.

For the entire bus trip I had rehearsed in my mind what I would say, but instead I just blurted it out. "I'm getting married!" I exclaimed happily holding out my left hand with the beautiful ring.

From the dining room, I could hear my Dad. "Bullshit!" is all he said.

"Well, I am." I said obstinately. This was just what I had expected and the very reason that I didn't want John with me. Why would I subject him to this reaction when he was an innocent in this scenario?

By the time dinner was over, they knew I was serious and they admitted that they liked John.

I remembered how excited I was to be marrying John and all the fun we had planning the wedding. No, it wasn't always bad. Our main social life was through the church. Pot luck dinners, inviting friends over for dinner and games, going to movies, it was a lot of fun.

We decided to have a baby the third year into the marriage. I started working part time and he had a good job at a local hospital. We were both really excited. Most of our friends were having kids at the same time. Sam was a joy and easy to take anywhere, a pleasant baby. John and I both doted on him and the first years with Sam were the happiest of our marriage. We took him to the park, baseball games and camping. I loved being a wife and mother.

Then things changed. John was in and out of work and I went back to work full time. With each job failure, John became more irritable. It got to where my stomach would begin to hurt riding the bus home each night, afraid of what confrontation would be awaiting me. This continued for a couple of years.

We set up an appointment with our Pastor for marriage counseling, but John didn't show up the first time. We made another appointment a few weeks later. I got to the appointment first.

"You know, Tina, no one is an innocent here. It takes two people in a marriage." Pastor Ed told me before John arrived.

Biting my lip, I fidgeted nervously. "I know."

There was a knock on the door. John walked in.

"Hi" Pastor and I said in unison.

John just looked from Pastor to me and then mumbled, "Hi".

"So, are we ready to get started?" Pastor asked as John closed the door.

"Who wants to start?"

I could feel the tension, so dense in the room, and couldn't speak.

"I will," John said glaring at me. "She won't fight!"

With that accusation, he shot up from the chair, threw his hat down on the floor and stormed out slamming the door.

I started to cry and looked over at Pastor. He just sat there with his mouth open in surprise. What just happened and what brought that on?

The failed counseling session was the only one we had. And John was right, I wouldn't fight, no, I had learned my lesson in Alaska that it was better not to fight a man. It seemed kind of ironic now, that I finally fought back. And fled.

Chapter 9

I arrived back at my apartment. It was an emotional day and I needed to do something physical to let off steam. I cleaned the apartment and packed up John's things. That really made the whole thing seem real. The act of cleaning the house gave me a feeling of some control over this life that was pulling apart at the seams. Sam and I are on our own. The thought of it humbled and scared me. I wanted to run back to the safety of my parent's house.

I put on some Beatle's music in an effort to lift my spirits and escape from the reality of it all. I just wanted to run away.

It was never my way to wallow in self-pity and I was not about to start now. If there ever was a time for a "plan B" this was it. After all I wasn't in this alone this time, Sam needed to feel like everything would be okay. There just wasn't any way that I could let myself fall apart, not with him depending on me.

My emotions were overwhelming me and I scrubbed the cabinets so hard it was a wonder the finish didn't come off. The house was sparkling clean by the time I made dinner. Spaghetti and meatballs was Sam's favorite dish, great comfort food. I mixed the ground beef and bread crumbs with seasoning and put them in the oven to bake. Put the water on to boil and mixed up a batch of chocolate chip cookies. Sam seemed okay when he left for school, but, still, I wanted the apartment to feel comforting and safe when he got home.

It was four o'clock when I walked back to Rose's house. Sam was already there. He rushed over when he heard my voice and grabbed me for a hug. Rose offered to have us stay for dinner but I thanked her and told her I already had it started. Sam looked up at me.

"Where are we going to live, mom?"

"Well, we are going to stay right in the same apartment."

"Yay!" Sam and Matt sang in unison.

"Everything will be the same, honey. You can come here after school and wait for me to get home. That is, if it's okay with you, Rose."

"Of course it is! The boys love their time together, and Sam is a delightful boy."

"Thank you," I said with heartfelt gratitude.

We walked home with Sam chatting away about his day. He hummed a tune and worked on his homework while I finished making dinner. Without looking up, he asked, "Is dad coming back?"

"No, honey, no. He is not coming back. He is still your dad and you will be able to see him and spend time with him, but, he will not be living with us anymore. It's just you and me. Hope that's okay with you."

He just smiled and continued writing.

Chapter 10

"Where were you yesterday?" Jake asked. "I was sure I saw you in the lobby, but, Sarah said that you were ill."

I walked into Jake's office, closed the door and took a seat. I looked down at the floor as the tears filled my eyes. Jake came around from his desk and put his hand on my shoulder. The compassion in his eyes only made it harder for me to talk.

"What's wrong, Tina? Please tell me."

"My marriage is over. I hired a lawyer. You weren't seeing things, I was in the lobby yesterday, but my emotions were too raw for me to work. So I called the office and then went home."

"Do you need to go home now? It's okay, we can catch up on the project tomorrow."

"No, no, thanks. It would be better for me to just delve into my work and forget what happened. Please."

"Sure, sure, hey if you need to talk about it, I have a shoulder to spare. Just, please take care of yourself. How is Sam?"

"He's good, kids are resilient. In fact, I think he may even be a little relieved. Thanks for asking about him," walking slowly out the door I turned, "If you don't mind, I'm going to work in my office for a while."

Jake walked back behind his desk and sat down. He stared out his window wondering what happened. "Is this my fault? Tina had never let on that there were any problems in her marriage. What could John have done to bring such an abrupt ending? And, what should I do now? I am clearly attracted to this woman and my marriage is on shaky ground. No matter how hard I try, I just can't bring myself to trust Mindy. The thought that she might be in my bed with someone else while I'm working is always in the back of my mind. This news just makes me want to give up trying to save my marriage and come clean about my feelings for Tina." He couldn't concentrate with so many thoughts running through his head.

"But that isn't a good idea. No matter what, Tina will need some time to get over this," he thought. He needed to be respectful of her and give her time.

Chapter 11

Sam seemed happier with his dad gone. More relaxed. He even did his homework without being asked. Now he would invite Matt over to our place, he laughed more. Just seeing the change in him made me feel better and more certain that I made the right choice. How could I have been so blind on how the tension was affecting him? I bought a used car. We had more independence and freedom than ever before. Life was good.

Work was going great too. Jake and I still worked side by side most days. He had stayed true to his word. We kept everything business like. After all he was still married. Most afternoons were filled with laughter as we went over the notes and planned our next move. Sometimes his leg brushed up against mine as we huddled over the books or our shoulders would touch, neither of us moved apart.

Several months had passed, it was a Friday when Jake walked me to the door of his office. The outer office was dark, everyone had gone home. As I started to walk out, I felt his hand on my shoulder.

In a hoarse voice, thick with desire, he whispered, "Can I come over for a cup of tea tonight?" His hot breath sliding across my ear, sexy and sensual, ignited the desire that instantly soared through my body. It took every ounce of self-control to refuse, when every bone in my body wanted to grab him right there and melt into his arms. Feel the lusciousness of his hot, wet lips. He simply smiled. The look of amusement in his eyes betrayed his confidence that I would succumb to his charms in the end.

Each week, on Friday, he would come up behind me, the hot moist breath caressing my ears, asking the same question. The heat igniting in my body, weakening my resolve. With my refusal, the same knowing grin would appear. I think he actually liked that I didn't fall prey to him so easily. The excitement of the hunt. It had become our private ritual.

Chapter 12

The campaign was a huge success. We raised a million dollars for the fire department. The Agency and Fire Department were both pleased and surprised. In celebration, a gala dinner was planned. It was a black tie affair to be held at the Country Club. Jake, Mike and I would be the guests of honor.

I wore a black mermaid style dress, tight at the knees and then flaring out. It was low cut and covered in lace, plunging in the back. My curly black hair was swooped up on one side showing off my diamond earrings and necklace. Jake arrived with his wife, Mindy. She was in a champagne colored dress with gold jewelry to show off her blonde hair. He looked exquisite in his black tuxedo as it hung perfectly on his tall, fit frame. His golden hair and blue eyes seemed to sparkle as he took in the room. There was an audible gasp from the woman beside me as she caught sight of him.

We were seated at the head table along with Mike and the fire chief and their wives. Jake sat across from me and next to Mindy. I took a bite of my food and felt something gently rub my leg and reach up over my knee. What? Glancing across the table, Jake's head was tilted down. He lifted his eyes to look at me and a smile graced his lips. The softness of Jake's hands touching my skin, going ever higher swelled me with desire and instantly flushed my cheeks.

Just then his wife remarked, "Are you okay, Tina, you look all red, like you're blushing?"

"Just hot." I managed to squeak out glancing at Jake. Jake kept his eyes down, knowing if he looked at me the secret would be exposed.

The memory of that night brought a smile to my heart.

Even now stroking his golden hair, these thoughts had the power to fill me with desire. When I looked in his eyes, still seeing the man that he was, that he would always be to me. I bent down and kissed his lips, he awakened for an instant, the corners of his mouth turning up ever so slightly into the faintest of smiles.

"The next Friday, as he saddled up beside me and whispered the same question that he had asked time and again, "Can I come over for a cup of tea tonight?"

I turned and whispered in his ear, letting my lips brush ever so slightly against them, the hot breath gliding over and penetrating, "Yes."

His eyes got wide and so did his grin, "Really?"

The broad smile now revealing his innermost thoughts, was it conquest, success, desire, anticipation. No matter. My heart beat faster within my chest, what had I just done? Fear, trepidation, and excitement overwhelmed me as I walked out of his office, knees shaking. Fighting the urge to turn around.

I rushed home, we never set a time. I picked Sam up at Rose's, no time to chit chat. I made some dinner for Sam, though I couldn't eat. My stomach was filled with butterflies. What would the night ahead bring?

Chapter 13

The minutes passed like hours and still no knock on the door. Disappointed, I resigned myself to bed. Lying there, the sleep would not come. My body was on fire with desire for this man and my mind raced in all directions. What had happened? After 6 months of asking, why didn't he show up?

The knock at the door shattered the silence. I sat straight up and looked at the clock. One in the morning. What should I do? Surely it was much too late to let him in. I crept out of bed and parted the living room curtains ever so slightly. He was leaning against his corvette, looking up at the apartment, smiling. The moon shone only on him lighting him up in the darkness like a chiaroscuro painting. It was as if he was looking right at me and through me. Mesmerized, I stood there staring down at him.

Thinking back now, I realized it all could have ended that night. Bad timing. A burst of conscience. A withdrawn invitation.

Lying in bed I struggled with my thoughts as sleep evaded me. Wasn't I the one that always followed the rules, tried to do the right thing, the "good" girl. What was I thinking? Who was this person that I had become? What magnetic hold did this man have on me? Then, did I miss my one opportunity? I so hoped not. Inside my stomach was churning. The emotions from relief to panic, to sadness swept over me.

It was a normal Saturday. Sam was out playing with friends and I was busying myself around the house. My mind preoccupied with the previous night. Why didn't I just let him in? The ringing of the phone filled me with instant hope.

"Hello?"

"What happened last night?"

"Well, it was too late, I was in bed."

"Do you want to try again tonight? I promise it will be earlier."

I caught my breath. "Yes" is all I could say.

It was after Sam was asleep later that evening when Jake arrived at my door. As I opened it, he took me in his arms, held me tight and kissed me. A kiss as sweet as honey. My heart beat fast within my breast as I tried to catch my breath. His taste, his touch set me ablaze as I had never known before. A way that I wanted to go on forever. But, wait!

"What about your wife? I don't want to hurt anyone."

"Don't worry about that, it doesn't matter. You don't need to know all that right now, later, trust me."

I melted into his arms as he lifted me ever so gently and carried me to the bedroom. Our breath mingled as his soft lips encircled mine. Slowly he unbuttoned my blouse one button at a time, grazing my breasts with his fingers. Silently he slipped my blouse off my shoulders as he bent down to kiss my neck. His fingers traced my body as he reached around to unsnap my bra. His mouth moved down from my neck and his tongue slid down my body, waves of electricity ran through me. I started to quiver with anticipation and desire.

His tongue left a warm, wet trail as it continued to explore. His hands went to the button on my jeans and he hesitated. Looking into my eyes as if asking for permission. He pressed his body against mine and I could feel his desire, his need. I reached down and took his hands leading them to the zipper. We gazed into each other's eyes knowing there was no turning back now.

The tension that we felt for each other over the past months was exploding and there was no way to contain it.

My breath caught as I lifted his shirt over his head caressed the tight muscles of his abs and felt the strength in his biceps ripple under my touch. I leaned up and kissed his stomach as I unbuttoned his jeans and slowly brought the zipper down. He stood up, never taking his gaze from my eyes, and stepped out of his jeans. He bent down and kissed my neck. He lifted my hair and his hot breath danced on my ear as his tongue explored the curvature and crevice. The corners of his mouth ever so slightly forming a smile. He lifted me onto the bed and climbed on top of me. I could feel the hardness of his body as our lips met once more. The heat between us seared our bodies, he entered me and exploded as our needs were met. My mind was filled with a thousand thoughts and no thoughts at all.

We lay there, our bodies entwined, spent.

The memory of that first night quickened my breath and ignited the need within me. How can that still happen after twenty-four years? It just didn't seem right somehow. We need more time. This can't be it. He can't leave me, not yet.

Chapter 14

Jake stole away in the middle of the night to see me whenever he could. Sometimes the best we could do was to hold a glance from across the room. But every moment together was filled with bliss, longing, desire, and so much happiness. Sometimes at the office he would find a way to touch my hand or even steal a kiss. He became even dearer to me with every encounter, and I to him.

Things at Jake's home had grown worse. He no longer reacted to Mindy's threats to leave him and take his son. She had lost control over him and didn't understand why. Where did he go in the middle of the night after their son was asleep?

She hired a detective.

It was midnight and we had just finished making love and were basking in each other's arms. Suddenly the silence was broken by the ringing of the phone. As I picked up the receiver, all I heard was, "Send him home." Stunned I said, "What?" "Send him home." I hung up and looked at him.

"I think that was Mindy, she said for you to go home."

"I had better leave." Was all he said as he got up, dressed and kissed me. Before he had time to get downstairs, she was outside screaming.

"My husband is up there with that whore!" She bellowed. She was causing a scene in the night as one by one the neighbor's lights turned on and they parted their curtains to see what was happening.

Jake walked past her, "Go home. You're embarrassing yourself." He got in his corvette and drove away.

Jake wasn't at work the next morning. Sarah told me that he was working from home for the next few days. All day long he was on my mind, imagining the battles that were taking place in his house. What had I done?

Still he had promised me that their relationship was already broken. He told me that I was only the symptom, not the cause of their problems. Each time the phone rang, I so hoped it was him. Five o'clock came slowly with no word. In fact, I didn't hear from him at all for the next three days.

The fire department campaign was a huge success and now there were numerous thank you cards to be sent. Copious notes needed recorded on how we advertised and secured the donations. Notes on the various dinners and the attendees were added to the excel spreadsheets to facilitate re-creating the same results next year. It was tedious work. It had been such a joy sitting beside Jake typing this information and re-hashing the events. Now it seemed to be just boring paperwork and lonely.

Chapter 15

Sam was up and ready for school before I was out of the shower. He was in the kitchen making himself a peanut butter and jelly sandwich for his lunch. Humming to himself. The change in him was wonderful to see. He was happy, relaxed, we both were. It only made it more apparent that leaving his father was the right thing to do. We rode to school with him chattering on about all that he was going to do today. I dropped him off and headed for the office.

Pulling into the parking lot I noticed Jake's red corvette. Just the sight of it brought a smile to my face. When I opened the office door, I could hear his familiar boisterous laugh as he told Sarah a story. Her eyes were wide as he delivered the punch line and she burst into laughter. She looked over his shoulder at me. He turned around and flashed a broad smile at me.

"Hey, Tina, how are you this morning?" He beamed.

"Great, everything is great." I exclaimed.

"Well, I got some new ideas for the campaigns. Can you get us some coffee and come to my office as soon as you're settled in?"

"Sure, you got it."

Scurrying to my office, I hung up my coat, put my purse in the drawer and went to the kitchen. Sarah had already put the coffee on to brew. As I waited for it to finish, I smoothed my skirt and wondered what awaited me. Even still it was hard to keep the smile from my face. He sure looked happy.

I grabbed the two cups and headed to his office. Jake jumped out of his seat and hurried to open the door for me. My hands were shaking and the coffee was nearly spilling. He took them from me and set them on the desk. He had pulled a chair beside his at the desk, I walked over to sit down as he walked back and closed the door.

"Wait, Tina, before we sit there, I want to show you something over here in the file cabinet."

Getting up I walked over to the file cabinet in the corner. The one that wasn't visible from the glass door. Jake took me in his arms and kissed me and then he whispered in my ear.

"I left Mindy. Yesterday I found an apartment not far from the office. She isn't taking it very well, but I told her that I'm filing for divorce. Already got a lawyer. Our marriage has been over for years and it's time that that we end it so that we can both find some happiness again."

Those words were music to my ears. My eyes welled up and glistened as he stole one last quick kiss.

"We better get to work now, don't you think? How about I stop over tonight?"

Somehow those same numbers that seemed so tedious and boring yesterday were exciting and new today. Anyone passing the office would wonder why we both had such silly grins on our faces. We kept our relationship a secret at the office.

Chapter 16

Jake arrived at my place a little after nine, knowing that Sam would be in bed.

"What happened, Jake, I was so worried about you?"

"Mindy got home a few minutes after me that night. Charlie was fast asleep in the backseat. I carried him up to bed. When I got downstairs, Mindy had put all the jewelry I ever gave her in the center of the table. She said she didn't want them anymore." Jake said. "I put some coffee on knowing it was going to be a long night."

"Anyway," he continued. "Mindy told me that she had hired a detective to follow me and see where I went all of those nights. She was more than angry that I was with you. She was incredulous that I would take up with another woman and when I pointed out the hypocrisy in her words, she became enraged. I never told you our past before, Tina, but it seems to be the time to let you know the whole story."

"We lived in Colorado. I was just getting started in the advertising firm and working a lot of long days trying to make a name for myself and a life for the three of us. Mindy had a part time sales job and was feeling restless with all of the nights she spent alone. It wasn't long before her boss picked up on her unhappiness. They started meeting at a local hotel during lunch, even went away together under the guise of sales conferences. I was blind to it all. Then one day they decided it was foolish to spend the money on hotels when they could just as easily meet at our apartment. After all I was gone most of the time. It just so happened that was the day that I received my promotion and a huge raise. The raise that would finally enable us to have a better life and a house in the country. I rushed home to tell her the great news. But, it was a scene from a bad movie." Jake continued sadly.

"The house was strangely quiet. But then I heard moans coming from the master bedroom. I opened the door to find Mindy underneath her boss. When he saw me, he jumped out of bed, grabbed his clothes and went to the far end of the room. Afraid of what I might do, when he realized that my attention was not on him, but the person that was supposed to love me to death, my wife, he made his way around me and out the door. So you see, my marriage has been over for a long time. I have tried to forgive her, to move on from it, but it's no use."

"Maybe I should thank her, if not for her unfaithfulness, we would never have come to Pittsburgh and I wouldn't have met you."

I sat there listening to Jake's story wondering what that meant for us now.

"Mindy always threatened me with taking Charlie away. It was her way of controlling me. Remember, even when we first got together I told you I would never leave him. When her threats stopped working, she got curious and hired a detective. The trouble is, now that her free ride is gone, I'm not sure how desperate she will become or what she might do." He remarked. "You could be in danger."

This story was a lot to take in. It made me happy that I wasn't the cause of their breakup.
Still, anger and the attending violence was not a stranger to me and I didn't relish being the target of a woman scorned. Mindy couldn't be happy about losing her free ride and needing to return to work. She was no doubt a bit of a drama queen, didn't showing up in the middle of the night screaming in the street prove that? Seems like Jake and I both had a lot of baggage from our pasts.

Chapter 17

It only seemed right that I should come clean too, about what happened between John and me. After all, he also lost his easy ride. You never know how people will react in these types of situations, who they might decide to blame. I put a fresh pot of coffee on and we continued talking around the kitchen table.

"Okay, my friend, all the cards on the table." I began. "You can have the long version or the short version. But the gist of the story is that John and I were married for nine years. It wasn't easy. For most of the time, he didn't work. For one reason or another, he would end up getting fired or lose his temper and quit. I wanted lots of kids, but, needed to work. In fact, many times, I worked two jobs while John stayed at home. Rather than try harder to make our life good, John would blame everyone and everything for not being able to hold a job or get ahead. I was always making excuses for him and celebrating when he would get hired. At some point, I quit doing that. And when I told him that he was responsible, I became the enemy." I continued quietly. "That's when it all fell apart."

"There was always tension in the house, Sam never invited any friends over. John would lose his temper over the slightest thing and scream and shout and throw things. When he hit me, I decided to leave. Sam and I ran from the house to safety and I filed for divorce. John knew that was the one thing I would not tolerate."

Jake looked at me with sympathy. "Tina, I had no idea that you were dealing with this all of these months. I wish you would have told me."

"What could you have done, Jake? And to have you look at me with pity, well, I just couldn't take that. Things are so much better now, for Sam and me."

47

Chapter 18

"You see, I had been through that before." I continued. "I was married for six months back in 1974 to a man named Glenn."

"I met him at a Christian Coffeehouse. We spent the day together. When we got back to my place, he forced himself on me. If you feel the need to know the gory details, I can go into it, but I would rather leave it at that for now."

"No, Tina, that is okay. I know this must be hard for you." Jake said kindly.

"In those days I was very religious and a black and white thinker. The church stressed that if you had sex, you were united with that person. I took that to heart and continued to see him, date him. I felt that was the right thing to do. Anyway after a while he decided to move to Denver to live with his friend. He didn't ask me to go and it broke my heart. He went off to Denver and I started working at the coffeehouse. I had already dropped out of art school."

"Would you like more coffee?" I interrupted myself. Taking a little time to catch my breath.

"Sure, give me a warmer." He smiled.

I took a deep breath and continued. "I loved working at the coffeehouse bussing tables or making hoagies. Terry, the manager, was a very interesting man and we would spend many hours wiping the tables talking about life. I had a lot to learn. It was then that a friend of Terry's, Tom, spotted me. He asked to be introduced and we started dating. Tom was tall and balding, with the brightest blue eyes and long dark lashes. He had a full time job as a laborer but on the side he played guitar and sang for church programs.

Tom knew Glenn and had heard all the stories about the domestic violence between Glenn and his former wife. Tom didn't trust Glenn at all and encouraged me to go to the doctor for a check up to be sure I didn't pick up any disease from him. Tom was always looking out for me.

We were together for three months when we went on a hike in South Park. It was a sunny Saturday in the middle of June. Along one of the trails, Tom lifted me on to a picnic table, got down on one knee and proposed. Caught up in the moment, I said yes and he placed a beautiful diamond ring on my finger.

By the time I got home panic had set in. He was a wonderful man, but it was just too soon for me. Tom had told everyone that he was going to propose and Monday morning they were all flocking around. I caught Tom alone and told him that I couldn't go through with it. He was crushed and I felt horrible hurting and embarrassing him like that. It is clear now that my life would have been totally different if only I had followed through and married him.

But, as fate would have it, a month later Glenn came into town. He asked me to go back to Denver with him. My friends begged me not to go, "two wrongs don't make a right," they said. But I couldn't hear them, I was determined to follow through, after all we had been joined together. Isn't that what they told us in all the Bible Studies? I just wanted to do the right thing.

I called my parents and told them I was leaving that night. They weren't happy. They tried to talk me out of it and when it was clear that I was going, they asked me to come to their place. We had a silent dinner and then they drove Glenn and me to the airport.

Chapter 19

We got married that July in our living room in Denver with a Lutheran Pastor and four other people that I didn't know. A pink ruffled dress and a tray of cookies from Walmart completed the wedding celebration. After two months we decided to head for Alaska. Glenn was going to get a job on the pipeline. We packed up an old Buick. Glenn bought a 44 caliber rifle for protection and we started off on our journey."

"Listen, Jake, I know this is a long story. If you're bored, I can quit now. But I would really like to get it all out and be done with it. I've never told anyone this story but I want you to know where I'm coming from before we get more involved."

"Tina, I'm not bored. But I'm worried that this is too upsetting for you. Of course, I would like you to continue. I want to know everything about you. You have to know by now that I'm head over heels in love with you. Rest assured, there is nothing that you can tell me that would make me think less of you. I promise." Jake reached over and took my hand keeping a steady gaze into my eyes as he said this.

I looked into the deep pools of blue that were his eyes. The compassion and love that I saw reflected back at me was almost too much. I had to look away.

"Alright, where was I." I cleared my throat. "Oh, yes, it took us ten days to make it to Fairbanks. We drove along the Alaskan Highway which wasn't paved at the time. It was exciting to see bear, lynx and caribou along the sides of the road. We passed huts up in the mountains where the Eskimos lived. Their children would wave at us as we passed by. It was an adventure.

We rented an apartment in Fairbanks and secured jobs the first week. It was warm and sunny the day we arrived in mid-September, but, a couple days later it started to snow and never quit. Then Glenn lost his job.

He was angry and irritated, things weren't turning out the way he planned.

It was on a snowy Saturday in October. He came in to the apartment and started yelling at me.

"Pack your bags." He screamed throwing my suitcase to the ground and dumping my clothes in it.

It wasn't clear why he was doing this but it made me mad too.

"No!" I screamed back at him.

With that he reached out and grabbed me around the neck. He lifted me off the ground, my legs dangling in the air as he held me by the throat and squeezed. His eyes looked like that of a mad man, open much too wide and filled with hate. A voice in my head told me to cough. But I didn't need to cough, I was stunned. The voice persisted in a more urgent tone now, cough! I pretended to cough as best I could with him squeezing my wind pipe. At the sound of my cough, he looked surprised. His eyes went back to normal and he dropped me and ran from the apartment.

He was contrite when he came back to the apartment. I was weary of him, not sure what had happened or why. Things calmed down for a few weeks. Glenn had gotten another job at a warehouse.

Chapter 20

We had two new neighbors from Maryland, Bob and Wayne. They had traveled to Fairbanks in hopes of getting a job on the pipeline. They used to come over to kill time in the evening. They were nice guys, but Wayne would wink at me when Glenn wasn't looking, I didn't trust him.

Glenn started going out with them in the evenings leaving me alone. Thousands of miles from any family or friends, I felt isolated.

Glenn and my relationship continued to get worse. I went to work each day not knowing what the night would hold when I got home.

One night in early December he went out, I didn't know where. It got to be late and I went to sleep. He returned at 2:00 in the morning.

Storming into the bedroom he pushed me from the bed. I fell to the floor.

"Get out of here!" he screamed kicking at me.

"No, I'm not leaving. What's wrong?"

Glenn grabbed the rifle from the corner, pointed it at me and screamed again, louder this time, "I said get out of here!"

With that he turned the rifle around and swung it at me just missing my face and connecting with my shoulder. The pain shot down my arm. I jumped up grabbed my coat and ran from the apartment.

At that time of night there was nowhere to go. The city was always teeming with men fresh off the pipeline up north, drunk and looking for women. It wasn't a safe place for a twenty one year old girl to be out in the middle of the night.

I ran across the street to the hotel. The desk clerk let me use the phone to call Pittsburgh collect. I called my sister, Donna, and told her that Glenn had held me at gun point and that I was afraid. Donna was going to try to get some money together to send me so I could come home. She wanted to tell my parents what was happening, but I made her promise not to. The desk clerk listened but didn't say anything.

After hanging up, I went in to the bar area. I asked the waitress how late they were open and if there was any place open all night. She said there was one, but it was across town. Not an option to walk to at this time of night.

Meanwhile the man sitting next to me at the bar struck up a conversation. I was 21 and he was a little older, maybe 25. His name was David. He was a kind man, saw that I was visibly upset and asked me what was wrong. After I told him what had happened, he volunteered to go to the apartment and talk to Glenn. I blurted out, "No, he'll kill you!" Then I thought to myself, what a drama queen. We stayed in the bar talking until closing time. Then he asked me what I was going to do. When I said I didn't know, he said that I could stay in his room that night. I was grateful for his kindness.

There was a large man at the end of the bar. He had been listening to our conversation all night and staring at me. I noticed him because he made me feel uncomfortable.

David told me his room number. He left the bar first and said that he would leave the door unlocked for me. As I exited the bar the desk clerk came up to me, "Look, I can set you up for a room for the night. You don't have to pay. I just want you to be safe."

"Thanks, that is kind of you, but I actually have a room right now."

I walked down the hallway and opened the door, when I turned around, the other man from the bar had followed me. He stuck his foot in the door and had an evil grin on his face. I shouted out, "David." With that the man at the door chuckled, pulled his foot out and went on his way.

Already upset by the events of the night, this man following me made me feel even more vulnerable. What would have happened if I was in the room alone? I started to cry.

David came out of his bedroom and handed me a box of tissues because I wouldn't quit crying. He gave me blankets for the couch and went back in his room and shut the door. I never saw him again.

Chapter 21

The next morning I got up and went to the apartment. I opened the door and was face to face with the 44.

"I thought that you would bring the police or some guy with you. I was ready to shoot them." Glenn sneered, confirming what I had told David and wondering where that thought had come from.

That is when I learned not to fight back, so, you see, John was right in his accusation. The next time Glenn came home in the middle of the night and ordered me to get up and leave the apartment, I simply got out of bed, quietly got dressed, buttoned my coat, raised my collar against the wind and walked to the nearest diner. I ordered a cup of hot tea.

"What are you doing out at this time of night?" The waiter inquired.

"Well, the truth is, I have nowhere to go. You're open all night aren't you? My husband just kicked me out." I remarked sadly.

"I am. But, sit here a minute, I'll be right back."

With that he walked into the back room, I could hear the muffled sound of his conversation. He returned with a smile on his face.

"No worries. I just spoke with Reverend Umphrey from the Assembly of God Church. He's on his way to get you. There are a group of missionaries staying in his church tonight and there's an empty cot that has your name on it."

"Gee, thanks, that's totally unexpected."

Within fifteen minutes, Reverend Umphrey arrived. "Come on with me, my friend,"

I followed him out to the car and we drove a short distance to his church. Everyone was asleep when we got there.

"Here is a cot and blankets. The showers are down the hall. Help yourself and in the morning we're cooking breakfast, please join us." The reverend explained.

"You don't know how much I appreciate this, thank you so very much!" I said filled with gratitude for the warm place to sleep and the sanctuary of the church.

Chapter 22

And yet, I went back to the apartment the next day. Glenn had cooled off and life continued for a few more weeks.

Bob and Wayne came over for dinner. Bob had gotten a job on the pipeline and was leaving for Point Barrow. Glenn informed me that Wayne was going to move in with us. Wayne looked at me smiling. Now, we only had a one bedroom apartment and it felt like a set up. That was when I decided to head home to Pittsburgh.

The next morning at work I told my boss, Dale, what had happened. He agreed to drive me to the apartment and then to the airport.

Dale stood guard while I dumped drawers of clothes into my suitcase. At any moment, Glenn could burst through the door rifle in hand.

"Quickly, Tina, I really don't want to be face to face with the barrel of a 44." Dale prodded anxiously.

We left the door ajar as we ran down the steps to the car, no time to lock it. Snowflakes stuck to our hair and coats. The below zero air froze our throats and burned our lungs as we ran for the car. It had been snowing for the past couple days. We sped along the ice covered roads of Fairbanks to freedom.

The airport was filled with holiday travelers anxious to reach the "lower 48" and reunite with their families. Christmas carols drifted over our heads and Christmas trees adorned the vast space. Twinkling lights everywhere.

"A one way ticket to Pittsburgh please." I stood at the counter in dismay. "I'm $13 short for a stand by ticket."

"No worries," said Dale "I'll give you the $13 and then come with me so I can buy you a drink. You sure look like you need it."

I got the ticket and we headed for the lounge dodging travelers racing to their gates.

"Thanks, thanks for everything, Dale. I really appreciate it."

"Don't mention it, but I need to get back to work. Safe travels, Tina. Take care of yourself and good luck." He hugged me and then was gone.

The alcohol smoothed off some of the rough edges. I drank, relishing the warm dark liquid lost in my reverie of the last 6 months. I wasn't always afraid of Glenn, but then again, maybe I should have been."

"Wow, Tina, I'm speechless. I am so sorry that you had to go through that. I, I don't know what to say." Jake pulled me close to him in a warm hug and kissed the top of my head. "My dear woman." He held me tightly.

Chapter 23

Telling that story, the one that had been hidden deep inside of me for decades, was cleansing. It was like years of tension and sorrow was being purged from my body. Jake's gentle kindness was the key that opened the floodgates. Like a tidal wave the tears welled up and spilled over running down my cheeks. I buried my head in his chest sobbing.

When I caught my breath I whispered, "Jake, I just told you the hard part of the story. It's sad and disturbing, but we need to look at the other part, the amazing part."

"I was the recipient of extraordinary kindness! Now, I'm not going to tell you what to believe, but look at what happened. What was that voice that insisted that I cough and why did I exclaim to David that he would be killed, only to find out that Glenn was indeed planning to shoot any man that I brought to the apartment. Where did that come from? The waiter making a phone call, the reverend coming out in the middle of a snowy night to take in a stranger with no place to go.

The willingness of my boss to stand guard at the apartment while I packed, knowing that he could be putting himself in danger. It took me three days to get home and along the way a policeman ensured my safety by putting me in safe room for the evening and brought me breakfast in the morning, some airline employees bought me lunch and told me about asking for a hotel room when my flight was cancelled. This when I had only $3.00 in my pocket.

People that went out of their way to help a stranger. Do they even realize how they touched the life of a young girl in a strange city so far from home? How they kept me from harm and gave me strength and hope to face another day. They gave of themselves with no hope of repayment. Don't you see, Jake, this is the part I want to remember? Not the horror and cruelty of someone who was no doubt fighting their own great battles. No, it's more important to remember the kindness, the love and pass it on."

"Now you are amazing me, woman." Jake said, "How can you come out of all that and not be bitter, jaded by the experience?"

"It's taken a lot of years for me to be able to tell anyone this story, but what's the point in giving up my future to anger over the past? Now, with the trouble with John, I guess it brought it all up again. Thanks for listening. I wanted you to know it all, Jake. I'm a two-time loser and if you want to walk away, I understand." I said tentatively.

"Are you kidding? Why would I want to walk away? You have been through the wringer and you emerged a strong and confident woman who knows her mind and isn't afraid to walk away when the situation calls for it. A woman who is able to protect her son and herself. I admire that."

"Oh, Jake, you don't know how happy that makes me."

Jake lifted his coffee cup in a toast. "To us, and better days ahead."

Chapter 24

The next week Jake decided to buy a Harley. He showed up at my place looking sexy in his leather jacket and cowboy boots. Sam was spending the night at Matt's house.   We were standing at the cycle. He put the helmet on my head, brushed back my hair and leaned down to kiss me. When we looked up, Mindy was there in her car glaring at us. We hopped on the bike and sped off. She put her car in gear and raced after us. We speeded up. She speeded up. All along the winding hills of Pittsburgh, we raced with Mindy close on our tail. At one point, she was only inches from our bumper. It seemed that I could reach out and touch her car.

Jake sped down the hill to the South Side of the city. He found some side alleys that were too small for her car and somehow we ended up down where the three rivers meet. The water's edge was deserted that time of night. A few homeless people had built a fire and set up camp under one of the bridges. We had lost her. We got off of the bike and just looked at each other.

"What the hell was that about? She could have killed us! Can't you get a PFA so she will leave us alone?"

Before Jake could answer, the sound of squealing tires burst forth.   Mindy had picked up our trail and followed us down to the wharf, she was driving at high speed. She lost control and hit the guard rail, went air borne and flew into the murky river. We could barely see her in the darkness, the car was sinking fast.

"Oh no! Charlie!"

In a flash Jake tore off his cowboy boots and leather jacket and dove into the river.

He swam as fast as he could battling the downstream currents to reach the car.

At the same time, I grabbed my phone and called 911.

The River Rescue arrived quickly, speeding down the river, sirens blaring.

Within minutes the wharf was ablaze with fire trucks and ambulances. Scuba divers jumped into the river to free her from the vehicle.

I could see Jake come up for air periodically but the car was quickly disappearing from my sight.

The divers worked swiftly and freed Mindy from the wreckage and brought her to the shore. She was unconscious. She had swallowed a lot of water and wasn't breathing. They performed CPR on her and tried to revive her. After several attempts they were successful.

Jake came back up for air. The breath caught in my throat as I watched from the shore, helpless. "Jake, Jake!"

One of the divers grabbed Jake around the chest and dragged him back to shore, placing him next to Mindy.

He was spitting out the river water, heaving from the exertion. "You have to get my son!"

Jake crawled over to Mindy's side. Between breaths he gasped, "Is Charlie in the car?" Shaking her he screamed again, "Is Charlie in the car?" I ran to his side.

She looked at him, struggling with her own breath, a weak answer, "No, he is with my mother."

Those words hit him hard and he slumped into my arms sobbing, "Oh, thank God, Thank God!"

I lifted his face to mine and kissed him. "Thank goodness you're alright" as tears streamed down my face. We looked out onto the river. The car had already sunk to the bottom of the murky river no longer in view.

They loaded Mindy onto a gurney and rushed her to Allegheny General Hospital. The rescue team was confident that she would recover, but they were puzzled as to why she was driving at such break neck speed.

Chapter 25

Isn't it funny that our tombstones contain our birth date, a dash, and our date of death? But, our lives are lived in that dash – that parenthesis in eternity; that embodies all that we have been, all that we have done. As we live out each day the time can go slowly making us feel that we have forever, until we don't.

How do you say good-by to someone who loved you unconditionally? Indeed, who was the first person that you ever believed really loved you at all? How do you go on without him when the hole in your heart is a great chasm of emptiness and just breathing requires all of your strength and determination? This man who was your life and the breath of your existence.

All of the hours in between, ensconced in that dash. The moments spent together in complete contentment and love. What really constitutes a good life? Is it the spectacular vacations, the weddings, births, the major accomplishments? Or is it really the moments sitting hand in hand watching re-runs. Holding each other close through the night and waking up each morning in each other's arms. Isn't it the embodiment of all that life has to offer, the good, bad, happy and sad? All of it blending together day after day molding and shaping you into the person you become.

We were married a year after the high speed chase on a hot August night. The crickets chirping as dusk descended on the little wooden cottage in the park. Our close family and friends and of course our children celebrated with us. The old wooden structure was filled with the happy sound of music, dancing and laughter. The little girls looking like princesses in their Communion dresses carrying their bride dolls and the little boys, shirt tails hanging out as they climbed on the sliding boards. Alcohol flowing freely and the woods alive with conversation.

This is where we pledged our love to each other.   Could it really have been seventeen years ago? It seemed like only a moment.

Chapter 26

J ake stirred and my thoughts came back from my reverie of the past. It was getting late. I kissed him tenderly and brushed the hair from his eyes.

"Time to go upstairs, baby." I said.

He slowly sat up, careful not to disconnect the air tubes. He held my arm to steady himself and as he ascended the stairs, I walked behind him ever watchful in case his legs should falter. His breath heavy with the exertion. To him it felt like a steeper climb each time he made it.

I helped him into bed and tucked the covers around him. Even with the struggle the sweet smile never left his lips. That smile that I had loved over the years. His breath was ragged but he seemed comfortable.

I got into bed beside him. "Goodnight, sweetheart." I said, leaning over and kissing him goodnight.

"Remember, you were the best part of my life." He whispered as he slowly closed his eyes.

"And you mine, my love." I replied.

I snuggled into him and fell asleep feeling the warmth of his body.

It was only ten minutes later that I was awakened suddenly by the sound of a loud gasp of air.

"Jake, are you okay?" I asked in the darkness. Silence. A moment later another deep breath escaped his body and he was gone.

"Wait, Jake, wait, are you alright?" I looked at him in disbelief. This can't be happening. We aren't done yet. We need more time. Wait. I have more to tell you, wait!

I cradled Jake in my arms, kissed his head and stroked his hair as the tears began to flow. Disbelief and sadness swallowed me up.

"Are you still here? Are you still in the room? Come back! Don't go!"

Still in denial, I left the oxygen on as I called the hospice nurse.

"Something has happened." I said swallowing hard. "I think that my husband has passed away."

"I'm so sorry, I'm out at the airport and won't be able to get to you for an hour." The nurse apologized. "Are you okay?"

"Yes," I stammered. I sat there, holding him, in shock. I spent the hour kissing his head cradling him in my arms. Weeping.

The knock on the door startled me. I went down to let the nurse in. We walked slowly up the steps.

"Did you turn off the oxygen?" the nurse asked.

"No, I wasn't sure if I should."

She walked up the steps and over to Jake's side and checked for a pulse. "He's gone." With that she went back down the steps to the oxygen condenser and turned it off. The constant whirring stopped, leaving the house in complete silence. The two of us sat side by side on the divan facing the now vacant, empty shell of a body – a body that once was alive and brimming with life.

She engaged me in small talk and then asked if there was anyone that she could call to come over. "No," I replied. She called the funeral home and then sat with me talking, passing the time before they arrived.

At one point she stopped, looked over at the bed, "Hey Jake, just talking here," she said politely to him. Then she looked back at me, "Look at him, he looks like he's smiling, that doesn't usually happen. He looks happy and peaceful."

The hospice workers have a unique way of dealing with the dead. Almost as though they believe that the spirit of the person has not left at all. It is clear that they have seen many phenomenon that they can't explain. Or perhaps they just have a deep respect for life and the transformation from one life experience to the next.

How could it all be over? How could I ever sit on that sofa again? We never sat on there without touching one another, leaning against him while we watched a movie, falling asleep in the tenderness of his arms. His love pervaded every inch of the house. Evenings making dinner with him kissing the back of my neck while I chopped vegetables. Playing games with the kids, Christmas and birthday celebrations. So much laughter, so many kisses, so much love, so much life. It all still hung in the air, the weight of the loss heavy on my heart.

Chapter 27

When the funeral home attendants arrived the nurse took my hand and guided me downstairs to the dining room. The items for the craft show were carefully placed upon the dining table. Scenes of oceans, sunsets and sunrises. The bright oranges and blues defying the vast grayness that had over taken the house. Just that day, I had busied myself with this. Now I wished that I spent the day sitting with Jake on the sofa, and left the craft show items for another day. If I had only known it would be the last time, I would have never left his side.

"These paintings remind me of my home in the Philippines." She remarked.

"These paintings, creating them had filled our afternoons together each day since March. Jake and I would put on music and retire into the room on the top floor, more than likely sporting a cup of hot tea. It was there that we spent the hours creating these happy landscapes." I offered.

Those happy memories flooded my mind and escaped from my eyes unbidden. Could I ever pick up a paint brush again?

Movement in the living room caught my attention and I stopped mid-sentence, standing perfectly still as my eyes took in the scene of the man carrying the black zippered duffel bag. The bag that contained the mere shell of the man I loved for 24 years. The shell that once was inhabited by his beautiful spirit, the essence of who he was, now discarded, like a hermit crab walks away from his shell to seek a new one. And once where there was life and vibrancy, there remained only emptiness.

Like a deer in the headlights the scene stopped me in my tracks, unable to move, speak, unable to breathe.

Chapter 28

Afriend once said that the only way out of love is pain. The comment seemed so bleak at the time. But now, so true, as the life I loved came crashing down around me.

The memorial service was postponed until the following weekend. Allowing me more time to grieve in private, to wrap my head around the fact that he was gone.

Preparing the photo board, planning the service, and choosing the music filled my hours. The doves would be released to the tune of "What a Wonderful World". But, it was a world that would be a little less wonderful without him.

The church was filled to the brim with people who loved him, whose lives he had touched.

Isn't it funny how many people's lives we touch in our lifetimes? People that we don't even know are being profoundly affected by our smile, our kindness, a touch, a moment of compassion. Each of our lives sends out a ripple into the universe, a ripple that extends into infinity with each other person's ripple that it touches as they unite.

It is impossible to be present at someone's passing and not be profoundly changed. I was no different. "What happened to my sweet love?" was the question that burned so deeply within my soul, that spurred me on into the search to find some meaning to it all.

One of the elderly widows, Shirley, pulled me aside at the church the next day. "Have you felt him with you?" "What!" I exclaimed. "Have you felt him with you yet? Bob comes to me at night some times. I feel his presence and can actually feel his weight upon the bed." I had never heard of this. But now I ached for communication from my sweetheart.

A few days later I had a dream. We were making love, Jake looked up at me tenderly. The boyish grin that I had come to love graced his face. When I awoke, the feeling was real, the afterglow. It was as though the event was real. That he had transcended time and space to make love to me one more time. I lay there, tears streaming down my face. He always spoke to me of time travel, parallel universes – had he been right all along. Were people on the "other side" truly able to communicate with us. I would not tell anyone what happened, surely they would think me crazy, off the deep end. But, nevertheless, the smell of his cologne, the feel of his tender touch, the taste of his sweet kisses, lingered with me all day long. I bathed in the sunshine of his love once more.

Chapter 29

I held that dream in my heart, away from naysayers, wanting so much to believe it.

The icy fingers of winter arrived in Pittsburgh. Below freezing temperatures and treacherous roads held me captive in my home with only my breaking heart for company. More than once I turned to say something to Jake and was reminded again that I was alone and that he was gone forever. Night after night I spent curled up on the sofa wrapped in a warm afghan watching re-runs.

A commercial caught my eye. Match.com. I watched with curiosity as the testimonies of happy couples filled the screen. Maybe this was my answer. I booted up my computer. First week free. That sounded good to me.

I perused the steady stream of photos as they flashed on the screen marking them, yes, no or maybe. My wish list tall, slender, funny. That is when I saw Tom a retired teacher and part time opera singer with a full head of salt and pepper hair and wide smile. He seemed interesting and I favorited him. Ding. He favorited me back. A minute later he had sent me a message.

"Hey, my name is Tom, it looks like we favorited each other. Are you interested in messaging?"

"Sure. My name is Tina. How are you doing tonight?"

"Doing well. I see in your photos that you're a painter. They look very colorful."

"Yes, I mostly paint landscapes. I like the bright colors. I see that you sing opera. How long have you been doing that?"

"Oh, it has been a few years. I'm currently singing in the chorus for "The Barber of Seville. I retired three years ago from teaching the fifth grade. Singing occupies a lot of my time now."

"Sounds like a good second career. I've been retired for two years. Enjoying the freedom right now. But I'm thinking of finding some volunteer opportunities soon."

We messaged back and forth for three days. It was nice to have a break in the monotony that was my life.

"How about I give you my phone number? You can call me, would that be okay?" He offered.

"That seems like a good idea. I would like to hear your voice."

It seemed awkward talking to Tom. Jake and I were together for 24 years. A lot had changed in those years. Last time around everyone met face to face, at a nightclub or through a mutual friend. This online stuff was baffling. What was all this winking and sending virtual bouquets? The dating world had moved on to high tech and I felt like Alice falling through the looking glass.

Tom and I spoke for a few nights on the phone and set a luncheon date for the following week. I anticipated our meeting with excitement and dread.

Chapter 30

The next day the phone rang.

"Hi Tina, this is Mark. I was on the legal team at the agency. Remember me?"

"Of course I do. How are you Mark?"

"Great, great, thanks. Hey, I'm really sorry to hear about Jake. How are you holding up?"

"Hanging in there, thanks for asking."

"Guess you are wondering how I got your number. I spoke to Sarah. Figured the two of you were still friends since you were so close back then. Anyway, hope you don't mind. I was wondering if you would like to go out to dinner with me tonight. I know it's last minute so if you're busy, I understand."

Mark could hear my hesitation over the phone.

"No, no it isn't that. I'm just surprised, that's all. Um, sure, why not."

"That's wonderful. I'll pick you up at 7:00 then. Looking forward to it."

"Me too, see you in a few."

Mark and I had met the day I started working at the agency. Most mornings he would grab a cup of coffee and come to my office to shoot the breeze. We had an easy friendship. Now I wondered, was this a date or just two friends having dinner. It wasn't clear.

Not knowing what the plan was, I dressed in a pair of blue jeans, black pumps and a black silk blouse. I topped it off with a silver belt and silver earrings, necklace and bracelet.

Mark arrived at 7:00 wearing dark gray trousers and a navy button down shirt holding a bouquet of roses. He hugged me hello. Hmm, guess this is a date, I thought.

"Hope you like Chinese food. I made a reservation at a great place nearby called the Silk Road."

"That sounds nice, I know the place, good food."

He ordered three different entrees and we shared the variety. It had been over a year since we had spoken to each other but that didn't hinder the conversation. His wit was as quick as ever. He described the latest happenings at the office. I howled at his impersonations of Mike. It really made me miss going into work every day, the camaraderie. The time went by quickly.

"Hey, Tina, it's way too early to call it a night. How about we take in a movie. There is a new Johnny Depp film, Transcendence, playing at the Village Theater. What do you say? Want to go?"

"I love Johnny Depp and it is pretty early. Let's do it."

He paid the bill and we hopped into his Mercedes heading the twenty minutes to the Village Theater. The delicious aroma of the buttered popcorn beckoned us. We looked at each other at the same time, raising our eyebrows.

"We'll have a large popcorn, lots of butter, salt and two cokes." Mark told the clerk. "Oh heck, throw in a box of the junior mints too. Thanks."

We settled into the middle row as the previews began, happily munching on the popcorn and chocolate. It was a weeknight and only six other people were in the theater. Two elderly gentlemen moved into the row in front of us and to the right. Two old friends out for a movie.

The third preview began and I noticed some commotion between the two men. I poked Mark in the ribs and whispered.

"I think something is happening over there, look."

Mark glanced over just as one of the gentlemen jumped up knocking over his cane. It hit the floor with a loud bang. This caught everyone's attention. He stood up and grabbed the bag he brought with him his hands were shaking as he ruffled through it.

Just then we noticed the other man's head slump to one side. Mark jumped out of his chair and ran to them. Another gentleman from the back ran up. He said that he was a paramedic. The older man was unconscious and the paramedic began doing CPR on him.

I ran over to pick up the contents of the bag that had spilled all over the floor while another woman ran out of the theater to get the manager. Someone yelled up to the projectionist to stop the previews and turn on the house lights.

The elderly gentleman was trying to open the oxygen condenser that was feeding oxygen to his friend. He said that the battery had just died and he was trying to open the canister to put a new one in. His hands were shaking too much to be good for anything. He said that they were both in their eighties and had been friends for over fifty years.

"I need to call his wife." He mumbled. Tears pooled in his eyes. I took his hand in mine, "It will be okay," I said.

Finally the lights came on and the manager stepped into the theater.

"Sorry for the interruption in your movie folks. We will reimburse everyone and give you a free movie pass to use later. Right now, the ambulance is on its way. I am going to open the emergency door so they can get in."

She walked up to the two men. There was still no response from the elderly gentleman. He was leaning back in the seat his head just hanging to one side. His skin had turned gray. Mark and I stayed in there until the ambulance arrived. The paramedics entered the theater and immediately went to work. We decided to get out of their way and left the theater.

Mark put his arm around my shoulder. "Are you okay Tina? That was very disturbing."

"I'm okay, it just makes me feel really sad. Two good friends out for an evening. So sad."

"It is sad, we need to cheer ourselves up." Mark said. We passed my old haunt, The Grove. "Do you want to go dancing?"

"No, if you don't mind, I think that I would rather just go home right now. It has been a crazy night."

"Sure, Tina, whatever you like."

Mark turned right onto Grove Road and ascended the steep hill. He made a left at the shopping mall where we had just eaten dinner and caught the red light.

"I have a proposition for you." He said glancing at me and then quickly looking away again.

"Oh?" I said, intrigued.

"Look, Tina, you had to know that I liked you all of those years. Why do you think that I came down to get coffee and stop in your office every day? It was just that our timing was off. First you were married and I wasn't, then I was and you weren't, and then, once you met Jake, it was all over for me. You two were head over heels for each other, that's for sure. And, well, I know it's soon, but, I don't want to wait and lose my chance again. We're both free now. What do you say about giving me three months? Three months to see if it can work out for us. If it doesn't work out, at least we can say we tried. What do you think?" The light changed green and we started to move again.

I kept my eyes straight ahead. This isn't what I expected to happen tonight at all. My mind raced as I stared out the windshield. I had just made the date to meet Tom. Still, Mark and I had known each other a long time. It seemed a reasonable request. He was a nice looking man, kind and funny. I reasoned in my head. The silence must have seemed like forever for Mark.

Jake's gone and I'm lonely, what have I got to lose, it's only three months.

"Sure, Mark, sure. Let's see what happens." I said as we pulled in front of my house.

His smile went from ear to ear as he put the car in park and an audible sigh escaped his lips.

"It's going to be great Tina, you'll see." He said as he bounded out of the car and ran to open my door offering me his hand. Clearly excited by the prospect.

My heart was pounding. It felt great to be wanted, desirable. I hoped I did the right thing. He walked me to my door.

"I'm not going to ask you in, Mark. A lot happened tonight and I need some time to process it all."

"That's okay. I'll call you tomorrow." He gave me a quick kiss and a long hug. Turned and walked down the sidewalk. When he reached his car, he turned back to look at me and gave me a wink.

I closed the door and sunk to the floor. What had I done? I spoke to the silence, "Jake, I hope that you don't mind. It is just so lonely here without you. You know that no one will ever replace you, how could they? You're a tough act to follow. I still miss you so much." Tears pooled in my eyes at the thought of moving on, starting over.

Chapter 31

Then, what about Tom? I needed to tell him that things had changed.

I pulled out my cell phone, found Tom's number and hit call. The phone rang and the breath caught in my throat.

"Hello!" Tom's deep voice resonated through the phone. "This is a nice surprise!"

"Hello." I coughed. "Hello."

"How are you doing? It's really nice to hear from you!"

"Doing well, how about you?" I stammered.

"Doing well also. Just sitting here with a glass of wine watching an old movie. Sure would be nice if you were here with me."

"Aren't you sweet? Listen, Tom, do you mind if I'm direct?"

"No, not at all. What's on your mind, Tina?" He said softly.

"Well, listen, ummm, something has come up and I won't be able to meet you this week. You see, an old friend contacted me. We worked together for a really long time. Long story short, he just heard that Jake passed away. He asked me to give him three months to see if we can make it together. I told him yes. It doesn't feel like an outrageous request. So, in light of that, I think we should cancel our lunch date. So sorry, Tom."

"Look, Tina, I understand. You have been friends with him a long time. It seems reasonable, but, I have a proposition for you." He paused and I thought, "Didn't I just hear that phrase?"

"Let's meet each other tomorrow. How about lunch at Bahama Breeze in Robinson Town Center? It would be great to meet you in person after talking on the phone so many times. Then, let's set a date for three months from now, say, July 23. We can meet at the same restaurant at 1:00. If it works out for you and your friend, just don't show up. And, if I am involved with someone, I won't be there. Is it a deal?"

"Wow! That is just like my favorite Cary Grant movie, An Affair to Remember. How can I say no to that? It's so romantic! Yes, you have a deal!"

"I thought you might like that. Okay, so we're set. I will see you tomorrow at 1:00."

"Yes, okay. It sounds great." I hung up the phone and just sat there. What just happened? This day has gotten stranger by the minute.

It was a night's sleep full of fits and turns. My mind raced between all that happened with Mark, Tom. Finally the sun shone through the curtains a promise of a beautiful day. Anticipation and anxiety mixed within me causing my heart to race. The hot shower did little to calm my nerves.

"Let's see," I thought looking through my closet. "Something stylish, but slightly conservative that would show off my curves, but, not to revealing." I chose a pair of tight stone wash jeans, black silk shirt and black blazer. The look was completed with black high heeled boots and gold jewelry. Elegant, but understated. I ran some gel through my hair to tame the curls a bit, added a second coat of mascara and a few sprays of my favorite perfume, Passion by Elizabeth Taylor. Glancing in the mirror, I thought, perfect!

That part of the city was unfamiliar to me so I plugged the address into the GPS. This nervousness was two-fold: meeting Tom and driving on the highway for the first time in several years. Jake did all the driving and the thought of merging and high speeds was unnerving. Still, it was time to push myself, become independent.

Dancing into Destiny

The GPS led the way effortlessly and I arrived 15 minutes early, fiddling in the car to pass the time. After five minutes, I gave up and decided to just go in to the restaurant to wait. Who knows, maybe he'll be early too.

"Hi, welcome to Bahama Breeze! May I help you?" The hostess beamed.

"Not quite yet, thank you. I'm waiting for a friend. I'll just sit over here." I said walking towards the sofas to the right of the greeter's stand.

"That is perfectly fine, just let me know when you're ready to be seated."

"Will do."

I settled in, took out my cell phone and read some emails just to pass the time. Five minutes later I noticed someone through the glass. In an instant I knew it was Tom. He was 6'2", clean shaven, a full head of salt and pepper hair, and dark brown eyes wearing a deep purple button down shirt and light gray trousers with light brown oxfords. A sharp dresser. He smiled the moment he saw me, walked over and gave me a friendly hug.

"You look just like your picture!" We exclaimed at the same time causing us to break out in laughter.

The hostess looked over and smiled, "Guess you're ready to be seated now. Follow me please."

She led us to a cozy booth in the back of the restaurant. The place wasn't crowded at all.

"Get whatever you like, Tina, my treat. Would you like to start with a glass of wine?"

"Yes, that would be wonderful. Riesling for me please."

The waitress approached our table. "We would like two glasses of water with lemon and two glasses of Riesling please."

"Coming right up, and then I'll be back to take your order."

We silently perused the menu. "I think I'll have the tilapia with mango salsa, rice and broccoli. What are you going to have, Tom?"

"That's funny, I was going to order the same thing."

The waitress returned with our drinks and Tom ordered for the both of us.

"Okay, now that the business is taken care of, tell me something about yourself, Tina. What was your family like?"

"Well, there were five kids in my family, four girls and one boy. I'm the third daughter and middle child. Italian background, mom was a great cook, lots of pasta and homemade sauces. We all get along great together. How about you?"

"I have one younger brother, who lives in Florida now. We get along well also. My parents have passed away. Full Italian background as well. Did your family sit around the table talking after dinner?"

"Yes, dinner time was a big social time for us. We never did the seven fishes dinner on Christmas Eve for some reason, even though Dad always wanted to. Did you guys do that?"

"Oh yeah, every Christmas Eve. All of the aunts and uncles and cousins would come over. Most of them are gone now, but I still miss that. The house was always full of company and chatter."

"Ours too! I miss the loud chatter and lively conversation. It's great when my sister and brother come into town and we're all together again. It was a good childhood, really. A few ups and downs, but who doesn't have that."

"That's for sure, you have to keep it in perspective, right?"

"My dream is to go to Italy one day. I want to see the David and the Vatican, the Tuscan countryside. Maybe even do a wine tasting there."

"I'm going to Italy next month with my daughter and 10 of my cousins. We're going to look up some of the relatives that still live there. One of my cousins did our genealogy and contacted our distant relatives. Wow, if we had met sooner you could have gone with us."

82

Dancing into Destiny

"Is it your first time then?"

"Yes and I am really excited to share it with my daughter, she is seventeen and just graduated high school. I was older when we decided to have a child but she is my pride and joy. How about you, any children?"

"Yes, I have one son, Sam. He's married to a nice girl."

The waitress brought us more wine. The conversation continued to flow easily and three hours passed in a blink. The restaurant was beginning to get crowded for the dinner hour.

"I guess we had better clear out of here, give someone else our booth." Tom suggested.

"Yes, it seems that way." I said as Tom called the waitress over to get our check.

"Thanks for lunch, Tom. I had a good time, you're a most pleasant man and a great conversationalist."

"I enjoyed it as well, Tina. Let me walk you to your car."

Tom held the door open for me while we exited the restaurant. We walked quietly over to my silver Hyundai Elantra.

"Is this your car?" He asked.

"Yes, this is it." Tom started to laugh. He pointed at a silver Hyundai Elantra a few cars down.

"That is my car, looks like we have the same taste in vehicles."

He turned to me with a sad look on his face. "Guess this is it then."

"Yes," I said sadly, "I guess this is it."

He reached down and lifted my chin and kissed me tenderly. "Sure wish that I was going to see you again, Tina."

"Me too," I sighed clicking the button to unlock the door.

Tom reached down and opened the door for me.

I started to get in the car and then stopped and turned to look at him, "Okay, so July 23 at one right here, if we're both free, that is." I said.

"Absolutely, July 23, can't wait to see how this plays out. Nothing against the other guy, but, I hope you're here."

I got into the car, he closed the door and started to walk away. I put it in gear and looked out the window at him at the same time that he stopped, turned around and looked at me. One last wistful glance.

Chapter 32

Mark came over that evening bearing a gift of candy. He was very sweet that way. We spent the next couple of weeks going to dinner, dancing, even tried the movies again. He was always the perfect gentleman.

We decided to go to the Meadows Casino try our luck on the machines and dance to the smooth melodies of Dr. Zoot. The Meadows was an hour from my house and close to his. Mark made the long trek to pick me up and then turned right around and headed back to his neighborhood. The machines were kind to us and we actually won some money. The band started playing and we headed to the main stage area, ordered a couple of cocktails and hit the dance floor.

"I would like to take dance lessons." Mark stated. "Would you take some lessons with me? It would really be nice to know the proper way to dance."

"Sure, that would be fun, let's do it!"

We got back to my place late and he was tired. It seemed crazy for him to spend another hour on the road so I asked him if he wanted to stay. I showed him the guest bedroom and gave him some fresh towels.

I went into my bedroom and closed the door. I lay there in the darkness thinking about Mark and all the fun we had the last couple of weeks. He was handsome, charming and good company. I heard the door creak.

"Tina?" Mark knocked and stuck his head in through the door.

"Come in." I said nervously.

"Tina, I can't sleep knowing that you're over here." He said kneeling on the floor beside my bed. "You have to know by now how I feel about you."

I didn't say anything as he reached over and cradled my head in his hands lifting my lips to his in a slow sensual kiss. He pulled away and looked into my eyes. "Is this okay?"

"Yes," I whispered. After six months of celibacy my body felt like it was going to explode.

His fingers caressed my neck and arms gently gliding over my skin. They danced gently along the curve of my waist and down my legs sending shivers up my spine, I held my breath.

I could feel his ragged breath hot upon me.

Silently he lifted my silk tank top as his fingers ran across the mounds of my fleshy breasts and down to my navel. They circled and then traced around to my back and continued up the center of my spine. He slowly removed my shirt and found my lips again. His fingers continuing to explore.

"You don't know how long I have waited to do this, wanted to do this." He whispered breathlessly.

He lifted my hair and ran his tongue over my ears and down my neck. My body ached for him to continue. His tongue traced my clavicle and then found my breasts, at the anticipation of his touch they rose to attention. His tongue continued ever south as he grazed my thighs and my calves. He kissed each of my toes and then his fingers ran up my legs. They stopped at the waist band of my pajamas. He glanced up at me. That moment seemed to go on forever.

Then, he quietly stood up beside the bed. He reached down and gently removed the clothing from my body and I reached up to remove his as well. He was already hard and I could see the desire in his eyes by the moonlight that shown through the window.

He pulled me to the corner of the bed, and our bodies united exploding in pleasure and set free in a moment of ecstasy.

With that, he gently lifted me up and carried me to the top of the bed and the pillow as he climbed in beside me, cradling me in his arms and kissing me on the neck. We fell asleep entwined together.

The thought crossed my mind, does he know that only six months ago Jake had passed away on that very spot where he now lay sleeping? Would it matter to him? Does it matter to me? Somehow it didn't seem quite right.

Chapter 33

The next morning over breakfast Mark said that he wanted to show me the huge industrial building that he had built in Florida and the property on the lake where he planned to erect a beautiful house. We decided to take a two week vacation trip so I could check it out.

"You can help me design the house, Tina. With your decorating skills and artistic talent, we could build a heck of a house!"

Mark wanted to move to Florida full time and was sure once I saw it I would agree. But, I was resistant. I had built a great life in Pittsburgh. My family and wonderful friends were here. I couldn't fathom picking up and leaving them, not to mention, Sam. No way. My hesitation kicked Mark in to high gear on trying to persuade me.

Since Mark lived right off the main highway, we decided that I would drive to his house at 2:00 in the morning, leave my car in his garage and take his Mercedes to Florida. We did a "dry run" so I knew how to get there. He lived in the country and it would be hard to find his house in the darkness of the early morning without having some idea of where I was going.

When I arrived at his place, he already had his suitcase packed in the car and was sitting on the porch swing sipping coffee waiting for me. The moment he saw me he jumped off the swing and came running. He opened my door and helped me out, giving me a bear hug and a long kiss. He unloaded my bags and then pulled my car into the garage.

"I'm so excited Tina! It's going to be great, I can't wait for you to see my place you're going to love it!" Mark was always enthusiastic. That was one of the things that I really liked about him.

"Yes, it should be a fun trip."

"Do you need anything before we get going?"

"Nope, I am ready to head out."

The plan was to drive to Charlotte, North Carolina and stay in a Bed and Breakfast for the night. I had found a quaint little place in the center of town and booked the room for us online.

Something about driving in a car lends itself to conversation. We chatted easily as always. Somehow being together in such close, private quarters caused me to open up to Mark. I told him about my past and the problems that I had, the bad decisions I had made. If he was serious about the proposition he made, then he should know all the baggage. The stories didn't deter him at all.

In fact, they inspired him to open up to me as well about his failed marriage. He was one of the lucky ones with a fairy tale childhood. A father that was always around and supportive and a mother that showed plenty of love. He had a couple of sisters and one brother and they all got along. A year ago he had become the full time care giver to his father as his health failed. He moved in with his father and took care of all of his physical needs until his final day. He was close with his father and talking about him still pained him. We had that in common, our grief.

Charlotte was a quaint city with a town square called Independence Corner where the four statues Transportation, The Future, Commerce and Industry reside at the corner of Tryon and Trade Streets. This is the center of Uptown and seems to be the hub and heart of the city.

Our Bed and Breakfast was one street over. It was a charming building green with cream trim. An Artist Market stood across the street. Mark suggested that we take our bags to our room and then visit the market before it closed for the day, then we could grab dinner.

The market was bustling with wall to wall people as we snaked around to see all the various arts and crafts works from the local artists. We were able to peruse for an hour before it closed for the night. Weary from the hours of driving and knowing we had a long drive in front of us again tomorrow, we decided to eat at a local diner and turn in early.

Two weeks is a long time to be with someone 24/7. Maybe it was the heavy weight of forever that hung over everything that happened. Maybe it was just too soon for me to even consider a permanent relationship. Maybe it was the pressure to leave the life that I built and the people I loved to start a new life far away. Maybe it was just too soon to take this sort of trip. Maybe Tom had something to do with it. Whatever the reason or combination of reasons, things fell apart on our long drive home.

The ride home was quiet. We stopped at a few road side attractions and to eat, and decided to drive straight through to Pittsburgh. We arrived home weary from the road. Mark loaded my suitcase into my car, gave me a hug and kiss goodbye and I drove off.

That would be the last time I saw him. The next day I texted Mark to say that it wasn't going to work out. I realize that was a coward's way out, and hoped that he would forgive me for that, but I just couldn't face the questioning of what went wrong.

Chapter 34

I t was tempting to call Tom and tell him that it didn't work out, that I was free. But, part of me needed to just be still. I knew that Mark had high hopes going in to the relationship and I felt terrible about calling it off.

Then there was the romance of the whole thing. If I called Tom now, well, we would start dating, but, it wouldn't be the same as if I waited to see if he would show up. Of course, waiting might mean that he would find someone else during that time. I certainly didn't expect him to wait around to see what I was doing. Romance won out, I would wait and meet him at the restaurant.

Finally July 23rd arrived. The morning brought a sense of excitement and anticipation. I wanted to look nice in case he did show up so I chose a black and white flowered maxi dress with black strappy sandals and did a second look at my hair and make-up before heading out.

"Well, this is it." I thought as I started the engine and tuned in the oldies station. It was 11:15, I should arrive there around noon, just on time.

Traffic was light and I got to Bahama Breeze around 11:55 and walked to the front door.

"Welcome to Bahama Breeze. May I seat you?" The hostess asked.

"No, not yet, thanks. I'm waiting for a friend." I responded heading once again for the sofa.

"Okay, just let me know when you're ready."

I took a seat on the sofa and fiddled with my phone again. The minutes went by slowly, 12:15, 12:30. I started to feel foolish sitting there. What was I thinking? Three months have passed. Of course Tom is with someone else.

12:40. Time to leave. Slowly I got up from the sofa and left the restaurant. Reaching my car, I opened the door and glanced around for a silver Hyundai Elantra, nothing. I got into the driver seat, closed the door and sadly sat staring out the windshield. Disappointed. I drove home with the radio off.

Two weeks passed without a word from Tom. Finally the suspense was killing me, just wanted to know the reason. I decided to send a text.

"Hi Tom. I don't want to bother you but I just have to know the end of the story. Why didn't you show up at the restaurant? Have you met someone else or were you just not interested?"

A few minutes passed.

"Hi Tina. I was there! Can I call you?"

"Really? Sure, sure give me a call."

My phone immediately began to ring.

"Tina, I so hoped that you would be there! I waited until 1:30 thinking that you were in a traffic delay." Tom exclaimed.

"What? I got there a little before noon and waited until 12:40. I was so disappointed."

"Tina, you had the time wrong. Remember we said 1:00?"

"Oh no, you're right. How could I have forgotten?"

"Well, I guess it turned out more like the movie than we thought." Tom laughed.

"So, I'm guessing that it didn't work out with the other guy, since you called me." Tom stated quizzically.

"No, no it didn't. Can we just leave it at that?"

"Sure, no problem. I'm just glad it didn't. Do you want to try again? We can meet at Bravos in Robinson. What do you say, tomorrow at noon?"

"That sounds like a good idea. Yes, I would like that. We can catch up then."

"It's a date. See you tomorrow. Goodnight, Tina, you made my night."

"Goodnight."

As I hung up the phone, I couldn't help but smile. It would be good to see Tom again. It felt like starting over, a lot had happened in the three months for me and no doubt for him as well.

The next morning I woke up with a spring in my step. Just the possibility of a new romance was intoxicating. The black and brown maxi skirt with a matching black top and spikey high heels was just the ticket for our second meeting. I wanted to make a good impression.

The GPS led me to a housing plan. What? I circled the streets with each house looking exactly the same. Finally I saw a man out walking his dog.

"Excuse me, sir? Can you tell me where the Bravo restaurant is?"

He pointed across an overgrown ravine to a new shopping center that apparently was built after my GPS was updated. He offered directions on the easiest way for me to get there. In Pittsburgh, with all the one way streets and road construction we have a saying that we laugh about, "you can't get there from here."

I followed his instructions and arrived at the restaurant only a few minutes late. Tom was already inside and as soon as he saw me, came to the door.

He grabbed me in his arms and hugged me lifting me off the floor and then settled in with a long, sweet kiss.

"It is so great to see you, Tina!" He exclaimed spinning me around.

We walked to our table with his arm around my shoulder, pulled the chair out for me and then pulled his chair close to my side. His smile was just as broad and bright as I remembered.

"Wow, it's so good to see you, Tom. If I remember correctly, you were going on a trip to Italy with your family. Tell me all about it."

Tom smiled, "I can't believe that you remember that. It was a wonderful trip. A trip of a lifetime really. Ten of us went, all my cousins and my daughter. We had done some work on our ancestry and found some distant relatives that still live there. One of my cousins contacted them in the small town of Palermo. When we got to their city, they opened their homes to us and served us the most delicious authentic Italian dinners. Homemade gnocchi, fried artichokes, fresh bread, tiramisu and wine lots and lots of wine. They welcomed us warmly."

"How nice that you were able to connect with them. Did they speak English?"

"Yes, most of them spoke English. Some of the older relatives could not, but the younger ones acted as translators. After our family visits, we headed off for the big three, Venice, Florence and Rome. It was all so beautiful. The fountains in Rome were plentiful and one more exquisite than the next. We got to see the Vatican, the Colosseum, and the Trevi Fountain, just to name a few sites. The David in Florence was amazing and the gondola ride in Venice was wonderful. The gondolier even sang to us – once he heard that I was an opera singer he asked me to sing with him as we traveled through the canals. It was just magical."

"That sounds like an incredible trip! I have wanted to go there for so many years and hearing you talk about it just ignites my desire again. I can just hear the sound of the singing echoing through the canals with the splashing of the oars in the water as back up. Wow!"

"Tina, you really need to fulfill that dream. Who knows maybe we can go together someday. I would definitely be up for going back."

"Oh, I hope to do just that. I have been studying Italian and I emailed my friend, Giuseppe, a professor at the University of Rome at least once a year for the past 20 years in hopes that I will get there and meet up with him."

"So, what about you, Tina? Are you okay?" he asked.

"Yes, well, my three months wasn't near as exciting as your trip. Mark and my relationship fell apart half way through the three months. We went to Florida for two weeks and it was just too much too soon. It felt like he had planned a life years ago and I was supposed to just fit into it. Anyway, I didn't call you sooner because the romance of our meeting was just too cool to rush. Isn't it funny, though, that we missed each other at the restaurant, mimicking the movie even more. Would you excuse me for a moment?"

I looked around to see where the restrooms were and made my way to the other end of the restaurant. The sign on the door said, uomo, I was puzzled. I pushed the door open. As soon as it opened, I saw a man standing at a urinal with his back to me. He glanced around as surprise showed on his face. Oh no!

"So sorry! Excuse me!" I quickly closed the door, looked around to see if anyone saw me and headed down the hall to what must be the ladies room thoroughly embarrassed.

When I got back to the table, I started laughing, "Well, so much for Italian lessons. I just went in to the men's room."

"What, couldn't you tell from the pictures on the doors?" Tom said laughing with me.

"I didn't look at the picture. I read the words."

Tom got tickets to the opera for my friend and me. We went to see the Barber of Seville. Luckily the English translation was projected above the stage so that we could follow the story. Tom was exquisite in the chorus, it was fun to watch him performing on stage. After the show, he took us to a local nightclub on Liberty Avenue with some other members of the cast. Drinks and conversation flowed effortlessly.

We dated a few more weeks, but it seemed that something was missing. He didn't like driving into the city and pretty soon the relationship just fizzled away.

Chapter 35

With yet another false start on romance, my thoughts went back to Jake. I knew no one could take his place, but would there never be anyone that could be a suitable partner.

I met a woman who was also a widow. She told me about a psychic in town, actually a medium. She said that this woman told her incredible things about her husband. I was intrigued and not a little bit scared.

I went online and made an appointment to meet with the psychic, then I cancelled it, then I made it again. Saturday, August 2. Our first wedding anniversary apart. The week before the appointment I was talking to Jake. "You better show up. I'm spending a lot of money on this and I need you to be there."

Each night I would get the heavy wooden box out and a screw driver, but I just couldn't bring myself to open it. The plan was to go to the psychic and then to the cottage in South Park where we got married and spread some of his ashes. Finally Friday night, I forced myself to remove the screws. Slowly I turned the first one, as it loosened and fell to the kitchen floor my heart raced. I carefully placed the screwdriver in the second screw and turned. It was tighter than the first and I had to use more of my might. Success, the screw turned and loosened. Before long I was able to lift the bottom of the box out exposing the sealed plastic bag. The musty smell filled my nostrils and tears burned my eyes. My hands shook as I opened the bag and removed a scoop of ashes and placed it into a small container. My head was spinning and my heart ached. Can this be it? Are we just reduced to this pint sized collection of ashes? Surely this can't be the whole story? Our lives must mean more than this.

Chapter 36

I awoke the next morning with trepidation. Soaping up in the shower, "Please meet me there today, please, Jake."

I drove to Brownsville Road and parked in front of the T Mobile store. I sat in the car for a moment collecting my nerve. Getting out, I closed the door, looked up to the window of her office and took a deep breath. Traffic was light and I was able to cross the road without dodging cars.

The door read, Marjorie Rivera, Medium and Psychic. My legs felt like lead as I ascended the stairs one step at a time. I reached the top and opened the door and entered the reception area. It was sparsely decorated with a desk and a few chairs against the wall.

"Hello, come on in." A sweet voice rang out cheerily.

I walked over to the open doorway. Marjorie was seated. She had short dark hair that framed her face and brought all of the attention to her deep brown eyes. Her face was full of light and love.

I pulled a chair out and sat down, my hands in my lap.

"Well, what do you want to do today? Do you want a tarot reading or do you want to contact someone?"

"Oh, umm, I don't know." I stammered nervously.

She took one look at me. Cocked her head to one side as if listening. "Oh, okay, we are going to contact someone."

"Okay," was all I could say.

"I see your aura and it is very pink, very loving. But there is a space inside where your heart would be. In that space is the infinity symbol. What I take from that is that you are afraid to love again. It is Spirit's way of telling me that you have a hole in your heart that only your husband could fill. You feel like he is gone, but he is not gone. He lives on the other side, the spirit world. So he really isn't gone at all. He makes me feel that he sits on the bed with you every night. He brushes your hair back and gives you kisses on your forehead. He says that he wants to be your last thought before you fall asleep and the first thought when you wake up each day."

"There is a song playing in my head. It's a Phil Collins song from 1987, "Against All Odds." Do you know the song?"

"No, but I have a Phil Collins CD in the car. I'll listen to it."

"Yes, he is impressing on me for you to listen to the song. 1987, he is making me feel that is important."

"That's when we met."

"I feel in many ways being drawn to South Park, like you guys have a connection to South Park. This is the first time that the park has come up in a reading. Does this mean anything to you?"

"Yes, that's where we got married. We used to go there to the same place every Valentine's Day. In fact, I'm going there after I leave here to spread some of his ashes around the cottage where we were married."

"He'll go with you. What he showed me, was my wedding, I got married in South Park too. He said to me, think of your wedding day. He is also making me feel thrilled about a pool, going to water."

"Oh, I'm going to St Martin and will put some of his ashes in the ocean. St Martin was our favorite island."

"I love that! He brought both places together where you will memorialize him. He's acknowledging your plan and agrees with it. He'll go with you. As he got to Heaven, he was not alone and he makes me feel that he was very loved and very well taken care of. He doesn't want you to worry for a single second about what It's like for him. He's very happy. He's telling me that he loves you and that he misses you."

"I'm feeling a corrosive effect, like he died of cancer, is this true?"

"I thought that he died from congestive heart failure, but when I opened the ashes this week I found an envelope with the death certificate in it. I never read it before, and yes, it was stated that the cause of death was lung cancer. That surprised me."

"He's confirming to me that it was cancer."

"He never told me that the cancer came back."

"There's one more thing that he wants to say to you. He wants me to tell you that it's okay for you to find another man to spend your life with. He says that he doesn't want to share you, but he knows that you need someone with you. He wants you to know that he never cheated on you."

"Marjorie," I say, "When it's my turn to go, I want Jake to come and get me."

"That's not out of the question, my dear" she says smiling.

Chapter 37

I walked out of her office overwhelmed by all that she had told me, anxious to find the song and listen to the words. It was only the week before that I had opened the CD case that used to be in Jake's car and had noticed the Phil Collins CD. Did we ever play that CD? I pulled out the bright colored jacket and looked at the song list, there it was. Hands shaking, I inserted the CD and skipped to number 7.

Jake was fond of shooting craps at the casino. More than once he would have me blow on the dice for luck while the crowd gathered around the table cheering him on. Jake had a "system". Sure, everyone in the casino thinks they have a system to beat the house. But, he did seem to be luckier than most as he amassed piles of cash. He was fond of saying that we "beat the odds" finding each other.

The silence in the car is pierced by Phil's tortured voice sharing the heartache of watching his love just leave with nothing he could do. Belting out the sorrow that all that's left is the empty space and nothing left to remind him of their love but the memory of her face. She was the only person that really knew him. He cries that there is so much more that he needs to say to her, the reasons why he did things. He realizes that it's against all odds that they will be back together. But still, to wait for her is all he can do and begs her to look, that he will be standing there, waiting.

These words pierce through my heart and gush down my cheeks. I sit paralyzed. My mind swimming from all that has happened in the last hour.

Can this be real? Still, sitting there listening to her was like hearing Jake talking to me. The words she used were words he used, this song, the same sentiments that he had expressed to me time and again. Maybe we're not reduced to a bag of ashes, maybe, just maybe there is more to us than that.

I pulled myself together, turned the key in the ignition and changed gears. The Stone Cottage in the park was only thirty minutes away. I hit replay. Each time listening more intently to the words and listening for the meaning, the meaning for me.

I approached the Cottage slowly looking for any signs that a wedding was taking place here on this bright sunny day. It was early in the morning and the Cottage appeared vacant. I pick up the small container of ashes and walked to the side entrance. The place is surrounded by trees. I carefully removed the cap and walked inconspicuously circling the building and allowing the breeze to pick up the ashes and swirling them, deposit them around the perimeter. I reserved a few for one more spot.

That being done, I stood back and let my mind's eye recreate that hot night in August. Transported back to the moment when we said "I do." I picture all of the guests and dancing, it's as though I can hear the murmur of conversation. And there, on the slight hillside, he stands in his black tuxedo holding me in his arms for the photographer. Like a dream that you can't quite remember, it is fleeting and then gone again.

The first February after our wedding was warm. On Valentine's Day, I bought some red and white balloons and packed a picnic basket with plates, napkins, Wise potato chips and two thermoses filled with hot tea.

"Jake, I have an idea. Let's go to the cottage where we got married for dinner. We can stop at Danny's Hoagies along the way."

"Really, it's bright and sunny but there is still a chill in the air."

"Please, it will be great fun. I love that place."

"Sure, Tina let's go."

We jumped in the car and headed down Route 88 towards the park. We stopped at Danny's and got an Italian hoagie for each of us. When we got to the cottage I spread the red and white checkered table cloth on the picnic table and poured each of us a cup of hot tea. We attached the balloons to the legs of the table.

"You're too much, Tina." Jake said laughing. "Who would think, a picnic in February in Pittsburgh?"

With that a tradition was born. Each year we would grab hoagies from Danny's and head to the parking lot at the Cottage. The second Valentine's Day was blustery. Snow encircled the van and accumulated on the ground. We stayed in the van with the heat on listening to music and munching on the sandwich and chips. Suddenly there was a knock on the side window and a bright light lit up the inside of the van.

"Hi officer," Jake said friendly, "We are just eating here."

"Oh," Said the officer. "I just wanted to be sure everything was alright over here. Not much call for a van to be parked here on such a winter's night. It caught my attention."

"We're just celebrating Valentine's Day. We got married here."

"Well, glad to see everything is fine, carry on. Happy Valentine's Day."

That happened every year. The police were always drawn to the van sitting in the pouring snow. Sometimes a few deer would go by rummaging for food.

I got in the car and turned one last time to face the cottage, then started the ignition. The final destination was a half mile down the road. I made the left off of Corrigan Drive and up the hillside across from the wave pool entrance to a grassy field surrounded by trees. Jake and I used to come here to sun bathe on the hot summer days. I pulled down the narrow path. Many lazy Sunday afternoons were spent here together.

My mind went back to one steamy August Sunday in particular. Jake started feeling a little amorous. As we lay on the blanket with the sun beating down on us, Jake started caressing my arms and legs. The gentle touch of his hands on my hot oiled skin and the sun's heat ignited our passion. We decided to retreat to the van for a quickie. We left the blankets on the ground and the music playing.

We got into the backseat Jake began kissing my neck and his tongue started to explore my ears while his hands reached behind me and unhooked my bikini top. He pulled me on top of him as his lips met mine in a long sensuous kiss. When our lips parted, I noticed the police car.

"O my ghosh, Jake! There's a policeman. Quick, help me put my top on!" Jake laughed as he helped me get my top on. He got out of the van.

"Hi officer. Can I help you?"

"Well, I saw the blanket and the music and no one around. I just wanted to make sure that everything was okay over here."

"Yes, we're fine. Just taking a break from the heat."

I got out of the van. "Hi officer. How are you today?"

"I'm fine, ma'am. Everything okay here?"

"Yes, yes it's great, just sunbathing."

"Okay then, I'll be on my way. Watch so you don't get too sunburn. Have a good day."

After the officer left, Jake looked at me, the mood broken.

"Thanks a lot, buddy!" We both burst into laughter. What was it with us and the police?

The memory made me smile as I sat in the grass holding the container with the remainder of the ashes.

"Jake, if you're still around me, please come to me. Please show me. Come as a beautiful butterfly, but don't touch me, you know how I am about bugs."

Just then a bright orange Monarch butterfly appears. It flies in a figure eight in and around my legs like an infinity symbol.

"Jake, is that you?"

It seems to stop in mid-air in front of me and then does one more figure eight around my legs. It rises and begins to fly beside me, but when I turn my head, it's gone as quickly as it had arrived.

I drove home in silence puzzling over the events of the day. Filled with hope that we do indeed live on and then wondering if I dare to believe it.

Chapter 38

That was the first contact that I made with Jake, but it wouldn't be the last.

When I entered the house I thought back to the confirmation that Marjorie gave me. The fact that Jake died from lung cancer and not his heart. I remembered driving him to the doctor and the sad look as he came out of the office. When I asked him what was wrong, he said nothing. But that was when he had me call the contractor to have a new roof put on. They were in the dining room and I heard him whisper to the man that he only had 6 months to live. He had not told me that. I thought he was just trying to get a good deal.

When the contractor left, I confronted him.

"Jake, I heard you tell him that you have only six months to live."

Jake looked at me and didn't say a word. Tears began rolling down his face.

"No, they don't know. You have been doing well. Don't believe him, don't."

That must have been the day that they told him the cancer had returned.

We had lived with the illness for seven years. It started with heart trouble. It was July 2007 the fiftieth year anniversary of the UFO landing in Roswell, New Mexico. Each year on our anniversary we would find a fun, unusual place to go, trying to make it to all fifty states. We decided it was a good time to visit New Mexico.

The week before our trip we were invited to a Bat Mitzvah in Squirrel Hill. The Synagogue was in a residential community and we had to park a couple of streets away. As we walked up a slight grade, I realized that Jake was having trouble breathing and walking. We made it to the service but he wanted to leave as soon as we said our congratulations.

We had no clue why he was having trouble. He had a stress test not long before and was able to keep walking on the treadmill much longer than they needed him too. This problem really hit us out of the blue. We decided to take our vacation anyway. I ordered a small compact car for the trip so that I could drive if necessary. Jake was feeling well when we got to the rental car station in Santa Fe and I forgot why I wanted a compact car, we upgraded.

He drove the four hours from Santa Fe to Roswell. It was the middle of the night. The road was absolutely deserted, nothing but red clay on either side of the road. No lights, no people, no traffic.

It looked like a scene from the old cowboy movies. Perfectly flat until a hill would jut out of the earth from nowhere.

We had missed the official celebration but were able to visit the Alien museum. The town had totally embraced the Alien culture. McDonald's play area was in the shape of a UFO. The street lights were Alien faces. Totally quirky and quaint.

The next day we decided to travel up the mountain to Taos the artist community. Jake tired of the walking quickly and found a seat on one of the benches. I could tell that something was wrong even though he didn't say anything.

"Let's go back to the hotel now Jake."

"I'm okay," he insisted.

"No, really, I am ready to go."

We made our way to the rental car and started down the winding mountain road. Before long it was clear that Jake was having trouble driving. He started to speed up just to get back. It was a harrowing drive as we descended the snaky highway. Finally we were at the bottom and at our hotel.

We got inside and put on a cup of tea. I could tell that Jake was having some trouble breathing. He was sitting on the chair with his head down.

106

"Look at your feet, Jake. They're so swollen. I think that we need to cut this short and go home."

"I'll be okay," he said again.

"No, Jake look at your feet, that can't be good. I'm going to call the airlines."

I looked up the number for Delta and gave them a call.

"We need to change our flight to go home today. My husband is ill."

"Okay, but we will have to charge you $100 per person for the change."

"I don't care. He's really ill and I need to get him home. How fast can we get a flight out of Albuquerque to Pittsburgh?"

"I can get you home as an emergency on American Airlines in two hours. Is that okay?"

"Yes, thank you. That gives us just enough time to get to the airport. Thank you so much."

I hung up, quickly put our clothes in the suitcase and we headed for the airport.

When we got there, Jake could barely walk inside. I ran ahead got a wheelchair and went to the parking lot to get him. In my haste and stress I forgot to take the brake off and was having a terrible time pushing him. Finally Jake realized what was going on and released the brake.

We got on the airplane and it took off right on time. It seemed like forever before we got to Pittsburgh. The airport was deserted this time of night but I found an abandoned wheelchair and was able to get Jake into it. We had brought the van to the airport. I couldn't drive a van. Jake got in the driver seat and even with his labored breathing he managed to get us home.

We weren't home for twenty minutes when he grew worse. I called the ambulance. They arrived quickly and started stabilizing him. I got into my car to drive to the hospital, but, one look at me and the EMT said that I had better ride with them. I hopped up into the ambulance and we took off racing to the hospital sirens blaring.

It was congestive heart failure, they never did determine what caused it, just blamed it on a virus. The strength and determination of this man was amazing. How in the world did he get us home safely while suffering such a severe attack?

Jake was a strong man. He fought the disease for seven years and didn't let it slow him down at all. We took cruises and road trips, we danced and laughed. There were severe bouts with hospital stays, but he always bounced back. That's why when the doctor gave him six months, I just couldn't accept it. But it seemed like it took the fight out of him.

The week that he passed he had rallied again, the comeback kid. He went to the dentist with me to see his friend. He went to my mother's for dinner. Thursday came along and the hospice nurse's visit.

"So tell me," he asked. "Does anyone ever get off of hospice?"

"No," she said bluntly. "No, don't ask me questions if you don't want to hear the answer."

That was it, the final blow. Just that fast, the hope was gone.

Two days later at the end of October 2013, he was gone.

Since then I have found out that, it is true, people don't come off of hospice, but many people live a very long time on hospice care. If only she would have expressed that sentiment to him. But then again you can't second guess, it was his time to leave his earthly shell behind and ascend into the spiritual realm once again.

And me, well I'm here, trying to build a life again amidst my sorrow. Plan B, starting over one more time. All the better for having known true love for 24 years, hanging on to the phrase, "Don't cry because it's over, smile because it happened."

Chapter 39

August 2015, two years into my new life. My sister and I decided to join in the community garage sale. She came over bright and early to help me set up. With all the tables adorned with what we hoped would look like special treasures, we decided to have a cocktail and some chips. The breakfast of champions.

People milled around stopping to browse, some spotting little trinkets to add to their collections. A blonde haired woman approached the yard. She perused one of my paintings for sale.

"This one is very nice. I like the bright colors." She remarked.

"Thanks, that's $25 if you're interested."

"I'm not sure yet. I just moved in down the road. Someone died in my house. My husband told me to stop talking about it. But, it's true. It isn't a problem, he's friendly. We don't have to worry."

"My husband died in this house." I offer.

"I know. He's standing right behind you."

My sister and I look at each other, "What?"

"I'm a psychic and he's standing right behind you."

"Really?"

"Yes," she says as she walks directly in front of me, staring into my eyes. "He never cheated on you."

Now I never even gave a thought that Jake would have cheated on me. But, that was very important to him to let me know that in his final days. I remembered him telling me that I was the only woman that he didn't cheat on and that it was very important to him that I know that. Here was this stranger telling me that.

"I do readings but I don't take any money for it. It's a gift to help people. Here is my name and number if you are ever interested." She said walking away.

At the edge of the walkway she turned around and smiling said, "Kisses on the forehead." With that she turned around and started laughing as she walked away.

My sister and I looked at each other. "What just happened here?"

"How crazy is that, she said just what Jake said to me and the same thing the other psychic said."

"Jake, I guess you are here." My sister and I raised our glasses to him amazed.

I treasure these moments in my heart, but, once again this wouldn't be the last time that I make contact with my beloved.

Chapter 40

Love is the only thing that is real. Love can reach across the edges of time and space. Perhaps when there is a love so strong, the earthly realm can't contain it. When two people are unwilling to let it go, unwilling to break the chain that links them together for eternity.

At least that's true for me. I don't want to say good-by to Jake or forget what he sounded like. Not willing to let those memories fade with the passage of time. So many times I wished that I had kept one of his messages on the answering machine so that I could hear his voice once more.

Four years had passed and a couple friends, Sarah and I planned a cruise on my favorite ship. A week in the Caribbean seemed like a great idea. Fun, sun, good food and good friends the perfect recipe for a great time. We walked up the gangway and entered the world of polished brass and lights. No matter how many times I had sailed on the Allure of the Sea, when I first entered its doors it always took my breath away. The beauty and excitement are intoxicating.

I glanced over at Sarah and could see the marvel in her eyes at this incredible vessel.

"Would you like a glass of champagne?" The waiter approached us.

"Yes, that would be wonderful!" We said in unison.

He smiled, handed us the glasses, and said, "Mademoiselles the cruise has started." Then he bowed and walked away.

This was the first time that Sarah had cruised and she had no idea what to expect. We giggled and tapped our glasses together.

"To a fun adventure!"

Sarah and I had remained friends, but we didn't have as much contact in the intervening years. After Jake and I got married, we spent time with the kids and on cruise vacations. Our life was full and though we got together for dinner parties with other couples, it was few and far between.

Sarah had gotten married to one of the lawyers from the firm. Things started out great for them but after a time she discovered that he cheated on her. Now she found herself alone again and re-discovering herself, wondering what she really wanted the rest of her life to be.

We were both looking at this cruise as a well needed time to get away – run away if you will.

The football shaped bar slowly descended from the eighth floor. It came to a halt and the doors clicked open.

"Let's hop on! It will take us to Central Park on the eighth floor and then we will only have to walk up two flights to our stateroom."

Sarah and I hopped on, champagne in hand. A steady stream of passengers followed us until the bar was filled to capacity. We looked over the side as it made the slow steady climb. When we reached the eighth floor, Sarah's jaw dropped. We were in the center of a lush park with trees and shrubs and beautiful flowers. The courtyard was open to the sky and was lined with scrumptious restaurants.

"Where are we?" She exclaimed. "It is so beautiful, how can this be in the center of a ship?"

"This is the Central Park neighborhood. Look up two flights, one of those is our cabin. Wait until you see it all lit up at night. Right over there is Giovanni's Table, my favorite place to eat on the ship."

We stepped off of the bar and onto the winding walkway. "I'm not sure which way to our cabin. Let's just pick a direction and when we get inside we can see which way to go."

Dancing into Destiny

We joined the throngs of people meandering around like lost sheep. We only had time to put our carry-on luggage on the bed and head back to the promenade. The muster drill would start shortly. The muster drill is a mandatory safety drill that takes place before the ship leaves the dock. Everyone is assigned a specific place to gather and are instructed on how to use the life jackets and the proper exit in case of an emergency.

Sarah and I found our way to the Champagne Bar, the designated meeting spot for people staying in cabins in our part of the ship. One of the crew members asked us to move closer together so that everyone could fit in the bar area. I moved in close to a tall dark man right in front of the bar.

"Do you mind if I stand here?" I asked politely.

He turned to look at me and a broad smile crossed his face. "Hello, luv. No problem at all. Me name's Ozzy, this here is Hugh."

"Hello, I'm Tina and this is Sarah. Do I detect a bit of a British accent?"

"Yes you do, me luv. We have been on the ship for a week already. Came over from the UK for a bit of holiday."

"We just arrived today. It's a beautiful ship, looking forward to a week of fun."

The captain came over the loud speaker. "Silence please everyone. Here is the international siren of distress, seven short sounds and then one long one. We do not anticipate any problems on the cruise, but, if you should hear the alarm sound, please come to your muster station right away."

The crew completed taking role call and dismissed us. "See you guys around. Have a great cruise"

Sarah and I went back to our cabin and changed into our swimsuits anxious to hit the hot tubs on the upper deck.

The next morning was the first port of call, Jamaica. We went to a high tea on a plantation on the hillside. The plantation was very ornate and towered over the city. A young man had built the plantation for his new bride many years ago when they arrived from Britain. Unfortunately, she died shortly after their arrival. He buried her in the basement and placed commemorative photos on the walls. A memorial to the heartbreak he felt on losing his new wife.

Our days were filled with sun bathing and the evenings with games, shows and more than a few hours in the casino. We passed the Latin night club and could hear the happy music of salsa dancing. We glanced inside and there were our new friends Ozzy and Hugh shaking their booty with a couple of beautiful women. When they saw us, we received the reward of a big smile and hand wave. It's funny, when you are on a cruise you usually make a couple of "friends for the week" and even though there are six thousand passengers, you run into the same people over and over again.

Seeing Ozzy and Hugh enjoying the dance brought to mind how Jake and I would dance the nights away. Even though I was having a great time with Sarah, it was still a little bitter sweet.

We headed to the casino and had a couple of lucky rounds on the slot machines, quit while we were ahead and then grabbed a cup of hot tea and fresh baked cookie from the all night deli and retreated to our room.

Sarah and I took our late night snack out to the balcony. The Central Park area below was twinkling with the white Christmas lights as the smooth sound of light jazz drifted up to us.

"This place is pure magic!" Sarah exclaimed.

"I'm glad that you're having a good time. I love it here."

"Aren't our two British friends a hoot? How about Ozzy in that bright red suit. He certainly has a vibrant personality and has some great dance moves in him."

"Well, he certainly does. He is one of those 'colorful characters' that you meet sometimes."

Sarah finished her tea and cookie and decided to go in and get ready for bed.

"I'm just going to sit out on the balcony for a bit longer, if you don't mind."

"Sure, that's fine, it's going to take me a little while anyway."

As I sat there watching, the twinkling lights seemed to be keeping time with the sweet music. My mind traveled back to all of the fun times that Jake and I had shared on this ship. I remembered him looking like a movie star in his tuxedo standing at the craps table and all the romantic evenings we spent dancing under the stars.

"Oh Jake, I miss being here with you, dancing with you." I thought.

Just then a monarch butterfly came out from the piping along the ceiling of the balcony. What's this? The beautiful orange and gold butterfly lit on the wall fluttering its wings ever so slowly.

"Jake, is that you?" I said quietly. With that the butterfly fluttered its wings once more. Then it flew to the ceiling right above my head. It stayed there moving ever so gently.

"Jake, I miss you so much. Thank you for being here." The butterfly took off and landed back on the wall opposite me. It stayed there for about twenty minutes. We both just stayed there on that balcony, neither moving, just enjoying the moment.

Finally the butterfly flew back up to the piping and with one last flutter of its wings disappeared again. I hadn't shared my butterfly stories with Sarah so I kept this to myself and dear to my heart. I didn't see it again during the cruise.

On the flight home Sarah and I re-hashed all the highlights of the cruise. It was like living a fairy tale for that week, now we were heading back to Pittsburgh and reality.

"You know," Sarah said, "This cruise showed me that we both need to get out more to just have fun. I was crushed when my marriage fell apart and I know you still miss Jake. But it's time that we picked ourselves up and get out there again. I heard of this national organization called Meet Up."

"Another dating sight?" I groaned.

"No, no this is a group that was organized to help people find other people with their same interests. For example, if you like to hike there is a group, if you like to go white water rafting, you join that group."

"Well, that sounds interesting."

"One of the meetings is a dance group. I saw that they will be at our local VFW next Sunday. There is a one hour dance lesson and then three hours of dancing. Let's go."

"That sounds intriguing, but I don't know how to dance, you know, the right way, I just freestyle."

"I'm sure that we can learn. What do you say?"

"Okay, sure, why not? Let's do it!"

Chapter 41

The month before the cruise I had a few false starts meeting men from the dating site. Usually it was just that they didn't look like their photo or we didn't have much in common but the last one I met unnerved me.

His name was Colin, he was a nurse anesthetist at a local hospital. We had gone out on two dates. He seemed nice enough but he didn't look at me when he spoke. I wrote it off as being shy. That's okay. We never spoke on the phone, only texted. When it came time for the third date, Colin asked me to go to his house on the other side of town and he would cook dinner for me.

I felt uncomfortable with that and mentioned it to one of my friends. Her response didn't help at all.

"Yeah, I'll see you on the milk carton."

I was already feeling uncomfortable and to have her voice that just sealed the deal. I texted him back and said that I didn't feel comfortable meeting him at his home, but, would be happy to meet him halfway to mine so he didn't have to drive so far. We decided to meet at an Italian restaurant.

I showed up at the restaurant and saw him in the lobby. I walked over to kiss him hello and he turned his head from me. Okay, clearly this man is upset that I wouldn't go to his house. The hostess seated us at a table.

He positioned his chair so that he was facing the opposite wall from me and refused to speak. I have a very low tolerance for pouting and wanted to leave, but, I thought, we have come all this way, let's just order.

The waitress came over and we ordered. Still he wasn't speaking to me and it was getting even more uncomfortable. When our food came, neither of us took more than a bite and we decided to leave. When we got outside he said, "Well, if we were at my place we could still be sitting and talking."

What, we weren't sitting and talking at all. We said good-by and both drove off. On the way home, I thought about what just happened and why he would be so upset about me not going to his house. This was just too weird.

When I got home, I sent him a text that it wasn't going to work out for the two of us and wished him well. Immediately my phone rang. It was him. I didn't pick up, there was nothing to say. He left a scathing message saying that he couldn't believe that I didn't pick up. That date did me in.

The next day I went to dinner with some friends and said I was done. Maybe I would get a dog. At any rate, I was not going to settle again.

"The next guy I go out with is going to be tall, at least 6' 2", dark, a cowboy with boots and black jeans, funny and kind."

That was right before we left for the cruise. I was happy that this group that Sarah was telling me about was not another dating sight. I needed a rest from that scene.

Chapter 42

Sarah and I were both excited and a bit nervous about going to the dance the next Sunday. What do people wear at them? Would we be able to learn the steps?

We decided to put our best foot forward and wear dresses and heels. Sarah always liked dark clothing so she picked out a little black dress with spaghetti straps and some black and white heels. The black dress only made her red hair stand out more. She looked stunning.

Always being a bit more flamboyant, I chose a bright red dress with a deep princess neckline. It hugged my curves in all the right places. I paired it up with red nail polish and lipstick and, of course, red high heels.

We were relieved when we entered the dance hall and discovered that everyone was dressed up. We paid our money and made our way to the first table. A couple of women were already seated and they greeted us with warm smiles.

"Is this your first time here?" One of them asked.

"Yes, we just heard about these dances and thought we would check them out." I volunteered.

"Well, the DJ teaches a one hour swing dance lesson first. We switch partners for the lesson so you will meet some of the guys right away. That is followed by three hours of dancing. Don't be shy, men ask the women and the women ask the men. We are all here to dance and just have a good time. It looks like he's ready to start the lesson now."

The DJ plugged in his microphone. "Alright everyone, we are going to start the lesson. How about I have all the men line up on this side, behind me, and all the ladies on the opposite side. Don't worry, after the initial move we'll pair up."

"I'm going to try to make this easy so that even the new people can jump right in and enjoy dancing tonight. Just follow me and my lovely assistant. Men start on your left leg, slow, slow, quick, quick. Women start on your right leg, mirroring us. Slow, slow, quick, quick. "

We repeated that move for a long time, until it became automatic.

"I think you've got it." The DJ said encouragingly. "Now grab a partner and form a circle and let's try the next steps."

Sarah and I hung back shyly. Finally two men walked over to us and offered us their hands.

I looked across the dance floor and down the row of men lined up. Glancing from one to the other until I saw him. My eyes seemed to fix on him unable to move. There he was, my cowboy. He stood 6'2", bright blue eyes, a clean shaven head, goatee, tight black tee shirt and jeans finished off with black leather cowboy boots. He was standing with his arms crossed in front of him. He looked like he would take charge of any situation that he was in. Exuding confidence and self-assurance.

My heart raced and my breath caught. Who was that guy! He glanced in my direction and I immediately turned away and began to blush, how long was I looking at him. I looked over at Sarah, raised my eyebrows and did a slight head nod in his direction. She nonchalantly looked over and then back at me, raised her eyebrows and mouthed the word, wow.

All of a sudden it was harder to concentrate on the dance moves.

"Okay," the DJ continued, "Now I'm going to teach you some turns. Men, raise your arm to her head if you want her to turn, just like this." He said as he gave his assistant the signal and she did a turn. "We are going to try that now. Here's what we do, introduce yourself to your partner and follow along with me. When I say change partners, ladies will thank their partner and move to their left in the circle and then introduce themselves to their new partner."

We continued to try the new dance steps moving to the next person in the circle. It felt like forever before I reached the mysterious cowboy.

"Hi, I'm Tina." I said shyly.

"Hey there, my name is Travis, pleased to meet you," he said as he took my hand in his. "Have you been here before?"

"No, this is my first time. Never did this dance before."

"I didn't think that I had seen you here before. Don't worry, you'll learn the steps, we were all new at some point. Most of the guys are pretty patient with the new dancers. Try to relax and just have fun."

He was so easy to follow that I felt like Ginger Rogers. We learned a few more steps continuing around the circle. Finally the dance floor was opened for social dancing. I so hoped that he would ask me.

Sarah and I both were asked to dance and the guys were helpful and kind with us muddling through. Travis was definitely popular. Before a dance was through, another woman was waiting to step right in. I gave up hope of having a dance with him, but then I looked up and saw him headed my way.

When he got in front of me, he bowed and offered me his hand. So gallant. I took his hand, "Thank you."

As he took the hand that I offered he spun me around and into his arms. He made it all seem easy as he swung me around the floor. He did a move where he came along side me, "Here I am." Then he went to the other side, "Me again." When he did this his eyes got so wide I just had to laugh. Of course, my laughing only encouraged him and he continued his antics.

I liked him already. Not only was he handsome and a terrific dancer but he made me laugh. The theme for the evening was Hawaii. The hostess announced that we were going to take a group photo. They had props over on a table at the entrance that could be used for the photo. She walked over to Travis and me.

"You look like you could use a good Lei." She said handing one to Travis.

"What does it show on my face?" He exclaimed and let out a boisterous laugh.

And in that moment, I was hooked.

He asked me to dance several times during the night and always we ended up laughing.

"What do you do for a living?" I asked.

"I drive an eighteen wheeler and teach yoga."

"Really, I am going to my first yoga class on Tuesday at the library."

"I saw that on the Meet Up website, maybe I'll meet you there, if that's okay?"

"That would be great."

We said good night at the end of the evening.

"See you Tuesday, he shouted after me."

"Yes, see you Tuesday."

As soon as we got in the car Sarah gave me the eye.

"Hmmm, you sure looked like you were having a good time in there."

"Oh, Sarah, I did. It was just like when I saw Jake for the first time. I looked over at the row of men and all I could think was – there's my cowboy! He's so funny and a terrific dancer." I gushed.

"Tina, you're so funny. And, what was this 'see you Tuesday' stuff all about?"

"Oh, he's a truck driver and he teaches yoga. I know, strange combination. But, I told him that I was going to the yoga class on Tuesday and he said he would meet me there."

"Wow, so it sounds like he's just as interested in you as you are in him. That's terrific."

"How about you, Sarah. Any sparks tonight."

"No, none for me. There were a couple of interesting men, that's for sure. I would like to come back and get to know some of them better. I had a great time. Everyone was so friendly."

"It was fun, thank you for thinking of this."

I went home on Cloud 9 and couldn't stop thinking of him. It would be great to see him on Tuesday and actually have time for a conversation. Maybe we could stop for coffee after the class. That would be nice.

Chapter 43

Tuesday finally arrived and I made my way to the Brentwood Library. I went over to one of the empty mats and sat cross legged. At 7:00 the instructor started the music and began showing us some poses. Travis wasn't there. Disappointment settled in on me, but I made the most of the class.

After class I walked home and called Sarah.

"O well, Travis didn't show up. Guess he had second thoughts. You know what's weird, he said that he saw it on the Meet Up website. I don't think that the Brentwood Library advertises on there."

"Here," Sarah said helpfully. "Let me pull that up." It took her a couple of moments. "Oh no, the yoga class on the website was at East Liberty Carnegie Library. Maybe he went there looking for you and thinks that you didn't show up. Yes, I see his picture on there as one of the registered people."

"Aw, man. I can't believe it. You know what, I'm going to look up his profile on there and send him a private message and tell him that I was at a different place. Gotta go."

I loaded up the computer and quickly clicked on the Meet Up website.

"Let's see, maybe if I search yoga. In seconds the class in East Liberty popped up. Travis was listed as one of the registered attendees. I clicked on his name and his picture appeared with a little box that read "send message." I did.

Hi Travis, I saw you on the yoga sign up for tonight. We both belong to Free and Almost Free. Hope you don't mind me contacting you. I had a great time dancing with you on Sunday at the VFW and found you to be a most interesting and fun man. Have a wonderful day, Tina.

Right after I sent it a message came up. "You've got mail."

Yeah, me too. Looked for you at yoga today. Let me know if you are going next time. Not too good on the computer, here's my number 4_____.

I decided to answer him right back.

Hi Travis, I was at the yoga at Brentwood Library. Sorry I wasn't clearer about that on Sunday. It was a meditation and stretching class, really calming. East Liberty doesn't appeal to me, maybe one of the other yoga meetings around town, or, if you want to meet for coffee sometime. Thanks for the number. My cell is, 4_____. So glad that you didn't mind me contacting you. Have a good day Tina.

Chapter 44

I was staying at my friend's house on Thursday night and leaving for Florida early Friday morning. Thursday came and he didn't call yet so I decided to bite the bullet and call him. I just met him, but, there was something about that guy, I didn't want to lose my chance with him. It just felt like we could have an awful lot of fun together. Just what I needed.

My friends and I had dinner and were sitting around chatting and I kept my cell phone close at hand, in case he would call. At 9:00 pm everyone decided to go to bed since we had an early flight. I told them I needed to make a phone call and went outside and dialed his number, nervous as a school girl.

"Yeah, this is Travis."

"Hi Travis, this is Tina."

"Well hello there!"

I could hear the smile in his voice.

"I'm leaving tomorrow for Florida for a week so I thought that I would give you a call. Do you have time to talk?"

"Sure do, I will just put you on speaker phone." Behind his voice, I could hear scuffling and a faint sound that I couldn't recognize. What was he doing?

All of a sudden I could hear loud crowing in the background. In fact, every time I laughed a rooster would crow. I started to laugh even harder.

"Where are you?"

"I'm feeding my chickens. That's one of the roosters that you hear. It must be something about your laugh that gets him all worked up. I have about 100 chickens and 10 roosters. I sell the eggs. They're Rhode Island Reds so the eggs are a brown color," he explained while his friendly rooster continued to crow.

We were on the phone for a couple of hours getting to know each other. I couldn't tell you what we talked about but the conversation flowed easily and freely. All the while my new buddy crowed away in the background.

"I'd better get in to bed or I won't want to get up tomorrow." I said, hating to break it off.

"Okay, how about I call you next week while you're on vacation, would that be okay?"

"That would be great! Okay, good-bye."

"Bye now, and Tina, I'm glad that you called."

I hung up the phone and went upstairs. Everyone else had been in bed for a while. I tried to quietly change clothes and put the sheets on the pull out couch.

"Who were you talking to for so long? I know it wasn't Sam." Elaine whispered.

"It's a guy I met on Sunday, he's so wonderful!" I gushed.

"Now, you have to tell me more than that." Elaine said, sitting up in bed and turning on the light.

"Oh, sorry, my head is spinning. We met at a dance and were supposed to meet up at a yoga class on Tuesday, but we went to two different places. I contacted him afterwards and he gave me his phone number. I was so nervous to call him. He's tall and handsome and looks like a cowboy, just what I'm looking for. He is so funny. He owns a farm with chickens, and a rooster kept crowing while we were talking. It's fast, I know, but, I'm smitten! He's supposed to call me while we're away."

"I'm really happy for you. It's good to see you smiling again, my friend."

"Thanks, you're a sweet friend. Not sure I will be able to sleep at all tonight." Truer words were never spoken. I didn't sleep a wink. I kept thinking of his deep sexy voice and those dark blue eyes and that silly rooster crowing away.

Chapter 45

Finally the morning came and we were all taking turns showering and getting ready to leave for the airport. My other two friends looked at me with question marks in their eyes.

"Okay, spill it sister, who were you on the phone with so long last night? And don't say it was Sam, we know better than that. We could hear you laughing out there."

"Busted! I met this guy at a dance on Sunday. I just looked across the room and there he was, tall, dark and handsome. And so funny, he just cracks me up. I was so nervous to call him, do you know what he said when I told him that? He said, "Why, I gave you my number?" That's just how he is a "straight shooter" if you know what I mean. I'm really taken with this one, girls."

"That's great, just don't get your heart broken, you have been through enough already."

"I'll try not to, but I have a feeling that he would be worth it."

The limo pulled in the drive and was honking his horn. We all grabbed our suitcases and headed out the door. I love the beach, this was the first time in my life I had mixed feelings about going.

Chapter 46

Before long the plane was landing in Ft Myers, Florida. We got the rental car and headed south to beautiful Marco Island. The South Seas Condominiums were ocean front and towered high above the other buildings. We were on the tenth floor and the balcony had a view of the ocean and the bay. It was a spacious condo with plenty of room for the four of us.

We got settled in and decided to head over to Nacho Mama's for some margaritas and nachos for dinner. The drinks were powerful and tasty and the nachos mile high with every topping you could imagine. We were famished from the day on the road and a bit giddy.

The week went by with girl talk, beaching, shopping and great restaurants. Sun every day. It was a wonderful time together. Each night I hoped that Travis would call but my phone was silent. As each of the girls called their husbands at night, I would ache to hear his voice.

Thursday came and we were to leave early Friday for the flight home.

"I am so disappointed that he didn't call me like he said he would."

"Well, maybe he had a good reason, Tina. Maybe something happened."

"Or maybe he just decided he wasn't interested." I said dejectedly.

"Sarah and I are going to an outside dance on Sunday. What if he's there? What should I do?"

"Well, you just walk up to him and say it's nice to see him again. Then you smile and walk away." Elaine suggested.

"Okay, that helps, at least I already have a thought of what to say, thanks."

On the flight home I played our conversation over in my mind. He sure seemed interested. Wasn't he the one that suggested he would call me on my vacation? I wonder what happened to change his mind. Maybe he met someone else. I let out an audible sigh at that prospect.

The limo was waiting for us as we descended the escalator in the Pittsburgh International Airport. We grabbed our luggage from the turnstile and headed back to Helen's house to get our cars and head for home. Hugs all around as we left each other.

"It was a great time." We all agreed.

"Hope he calls you," they hollered after me as I entered my car.

"Me too," I muttered holding back the tears. "Oh well," I said to myself, "at least I tried."

Chapter 47

As soon as I walked in the door my phone rang. My heart jumped hoping it was Travis, but, when I looked at the caller ID, it was Sarah.

"Hello."

"Hi Tina. How was your trip? Did Travis call while you were there?"

"The trip was great. You know how it is, a lot of good fun, food and girl talk. But, no, he didn't call. I'm really disappointed, but, I guess that's just how it goes sometimes. Bummer."

"Bummer is right! Heck, I thought that you would have something exciting to share with me. You know I'm living vicariously through you right now, right? Are you still going to the dance with me on Sunday?"

"Yes, get right back on that horse. I was just thinking of what I would say to him if he's there. You know, it could be a little awkward."

"Don't worry, Tina. It will work out, I just know it will."

"Thanks, Sarah. I just got in so I'm going to take a long hot bath and then unpack my suitcase. See you Sunday, at what, 2:00?"

"Yes, that would be perfect, so glad you're still going. This is a casual dance, since it's outside. Bye now and don't let it get you down too much, promise me, okay?"

"Okay, sure, I'll try. See you Sunday."

Chapter 48

Sunday morning I went through several outfits trying to find the perfect one for the dance. It was outside so it would be casual, but I still wanted to look nice. It was hard to find a pair of sandals that didn't have a rubber sole. I needed something that could slide across the dance floor. I finally found a pair that worked, I tried them out on the kitchen floor to be sure and put them in my shoe bag.

I settled on a pair of white capris, flowered tank top and white strappy sandals. Just perfect for a summer dance.

Sarah was there precisely at 2:00 honking her horn. Okay, this is it. I put on the sunglasses, grabbed my purse and shoe bag and headed out the door.

"To the dance!" Sarah said.

"To the dance!" I echoed. Inside my stomach was full of butterflies. Remembering Elaine's suggestion helped. Be polite and friendly and walk away. That's all you have to do, you can do this.

We arrived at the Mayernick Center on Camp Horne Road. The outside dance pavilion was across a small pedestrian bridge. As soon as we opened the car doors we could hear the music wafting down to us on the breeze. The parking lot was filled to the brim and we were lucky to find a spot.

We grabbed our gear and headed across the bridge. There was a slight hillside that we had to climb to get to the pavilion, good thing we wore flat shoes.

The place was packed with people. Some had brought picnic baskets with food to share. We saw a couple of chairs open at a table to the left. I sat down and took my shoes out of the bag. I put the first one on, buckled it and looked up -- straight into Travis's face two tables away.

As soon as he saw me a smile lit up his face. I waved and put my head down to get my other shoe. He was busy tying his dance shoes as well. I took my time all the while wondering what I should do.

Something was blocking the sun from me. I looked up. It was Travis. He towered over me.

"Hey, I tried to call you three times this week. Did you give me the wrong phone number?" he said laughing.

"No, I'm sure I gave you the right one. I wondered why you didn't call me."

"We'll check it later, right now, let's dance."

He took my hand and spun me onto the dance floor. When the song ended, he took me in his arms gave me a hug and a long sweet kiss.

"So glad that you're here. I was afraid I would never see you again."

"Me too," was all I managed to squeak out.

We danced every dance together as if no one existed in the whole world but us. Too quickly the night was over.

"Look I must have the wrong number. My phone is in my truck. I'm going to call you and see what happens."

He walked Sarah and me to her car. Then he sprinted to his truck and dialed my number. Nothing. He tried again. It didn't ring. He came over to the car.

"You call me."

The minute I dialed his phone sprung to life.

"Hmm, see, it's one number off. You would think the person I called would have called back to tell me I had the wrong number. I called three times and left messages."

"So sorry, Travis. I'm just glad that you were here today."

"Now that I have the right number, is it okay if I give you a call?" Travis asked hopefully.

"Of course."

Sarah got into her car to give us a moment. Travis put his arms around me.

"You just don't know how glad I am to see you. Drive carefully." With that he kissed me and opened the car door. "Take care Sarah. Nice to see you again. Good night ladies."

"See, it was all a misunderstanding and you were worried for nothing." Sarah said smiling. "He sure seemed happy to see you."

"Yes, he did. It never occurred to me that he could have the wrong number. I'm just glad it all worked out."

Travis, true to his word, called me that week. We made plans to meet at the VFW dance the following Sunday. The place where we first met.

Sarah and I arrived early so we had time to put on our dancing shoes before the lesson. During the last dance, my shoes fell apart. Luckily someone had duct tape in their truck, don't ask me why, but I was able to tape them together enough to get home. That inspired me to visit the dance supply store, The Tight Spot, and buy some real dance shoes. I knew this was one hobby that I wanted to keep going. Dancing filled me with joy.

The DJ called us all to the floor for the lesson. I looked around and didn't see Travis. It seemed that Travis tried to pack a lot into one day and sometimes his clock and time schedule didn't match everyone else's. Halfway through the lesson he breezed in. As soon as he saw me standing there, he flashed me a wink and a smile. My heart melted. How did he do that to me?

He positioned himself so that the next time we changed partners we were together. He spun me around as instructed and when we said thank you he gave me a quick squeeze.

The DJ showed us a few more moves, lowered the lights and opened the dance floor for the social dancing part of the evening. Travis made a bee line for me. He danced me into the far corner and stole a quick kiss.

Every once in a while someone would come over to cut in, but, we just pretended we didn't see them. We floated across the dance floor to the waltz. Feeling his arms enfold me was like heaven. I rested my head on his chest and listened to the beating of his heart. Everyone else disappeared as he transported me into pure bliss. I hadn't felt this happy for a long time.

I glanced across the floor to check on Sarah. She was with a handsome man who was gliding her across the floor as well. By the look on her face, I could tell that she was having a wonderful time. Our eyes met and she gave me a thumbs up and a smile.

Travis and I decided to leave the dance a little early so we danced our way over to where Sarah and her partner were.

"Hey, Sarah, Travis and I are going to leave now. Thanks for driving me down here. Are you okay with that?" I whispered sidling up to her.

"Oh sure, Tina, have fun. Kevin and I may be leaving soon as well. Have a great night." She gave me a quick hug and whispered in my ear. "I'll give you a call later."

Travis gave Sarah a hug good bye and took my hand. When we got to his truck, I noticed the passenger seat was filled with tools and sweatshirts.

Chapter 49

"**D**o you live in your truck?" I chided.

"Very funny, young lady. Give me a minute and I'll clear a space for you." He started putting the items in the back seat atop an already unending stack.

The truck was too high for me to climb into so I reached for the grab bar and with his help lifted myself up to the front seat. Travis closed the door and walked to his side.

"I'm just a couple of streets away. We will be there in five minutes." I said nervously.

We zigzagged a left then a right and ascended up a steep hill. As we rounded the top, I pointed to the left.

"That's me, over there. The purple and yellow house with the colorful flowers out front. I know, I'm the obnoxious neighbor."

"No, no, actually it looks charming and happy."

Travis backed into the driveway careful not to hit my car. The top of the cab was too high to fit under the carport so he was sticking out over the sidewalk a tad.

"That'll have to do for now." He said opening the door and coming over to my side.

He opened my door and I looked at how far down the sidewalk was. This thing was huge. Wordlessly he reached over, put my arms around his neck and lifted me out of the cab. I slid down his tall frame. Hmmm, I was liking this truck already.

He closed the door and took my arm as we walked to my front porch. My hand shook a little as I tried to put the key into the lock, wondering what was about to unfold.

"This is my humble abode." I said waving my arms around like Vanna White.

My eyes were drawn to the 8" x 10" photo of Jake in his tuxedo that sat on the mantle next to a stone angel statue and above the fire place. In a flash, the sorrow of moving on stabbed my heart.

Travis caught sight of the burgundy carpeting and rose colored walls adorned with all styles of paintings. If he noticed the 8" x 10" photo of Jake, he didn't mention it.

My thoughts were interrupted by the sound of Travis exclaiming, "Wow, your place is perfect!"

He spun me around to face him. Travis bent down to kiss me and the base of his hand brushed ever so slightly across my chest. The long sensuous kiss was filled with passion. We broke away and he looked at me, fire in his eyes.

"Oh, heck, woman!" He scooped me up in his arms, threw me over his shoulder and bounded up the steps two at a time.

I held my breath startled. This guy was unpredictable. I liked it.

He sat me down on the bed, bent over and looked into my eyes, hopeful, "Okay?"

My heart was pounding like a drum and I couldn't speak, all I could do was nod my head. An audible sigh escaped his lips.

He stood me up and began slow dancing with me all the while kissing my neck and caressing my arms. Humming in my ear.

We locked eyes and stood staring at each other for what seemed like an eternity. Then he gently lifted my curls and reached around for the zipper on the back of my dress. His fingers felt warm against my bare skin. As he lowered the zipper, one side of the silky material slid softly from my shoulder, then the other. The dress fell to the floor. I reached up and held on to him steadying myself as I stepped out of the fabric.

"You are so beautiful. I've been thinking about this moment, dreaming of it."

"Me too," I whispered finally able to speak.

Travis reached down and lifted his black t shirt over his head exposing the six pack abs and slightly hairy chest. His bulging muscles that had threatened to burst through his sleeves now set free. I gasped.

"You're magnificent."

He smiled, enjoying my admiration and lifted me up once more placing me on the bed. He slowly loosened his buckle and stepped out of his jeans watching me watching him. My mind went blank. Nothing existed but this moment, this time, together.

The world melted away.

Travis climbed onto the bed. His lips found mine, I parted them allowing his tongue to enter, explore. His fingers began to explore as well, softly gliding over my skin, making the hairs stand on end, giving me goose bumps. The passion built and I pulled him hard against me. He was gentle as he entered me and our desires ignited and then exploded into sweet release. We lay back on the bed, spent.

He pulled me close to him and I rested my head on his chest while his arms enfolded me. It felt like home.

"You know, the first moment I saw you something just clicked inside of me. It was like I knew you before. I can't explain it. But a warm feeling came over me and I just knew that I needed to get to know you. It seemed like you felt it too. I could see it in your eyes that night, your smile."

"Yes, Tina. I felt it too. I couldn't explain it either. There were lots of girls at the dances, but there was just something about you, something familiar. I really did think that you gave me the wrong number and that made me feel sad. I didn't want it to end like that. I didn't want it to end at all."

"Do you believe in re-incarnation? I mean, how do you explain this? Maybe, just maybe we were here before, in another place, another time. Just maybe we were lovers before and maybe that is why we were drawn to each other again. Oh no, please don't think I'm weird."

"Tina, I don't think you're weird, I know it. Ha ha, in a sort of wonderful way. Sorry, I can't resist teasing. But seriously, I know what you mean, and I don't pretend to understand it. All I know is that I'm happy you contacted me, my dear, and very happy we re-connected."

"Me, too, my love. I have a feeling that this is the beginning of something beautiful, something that I wouldn't want to miss for the world."

With that we drifted off to sleep basking in the deliciousness of new love.

Chapter 50

Travis and my relationship only got better with time. Sometimes it seems that love is easier when you are older. You already made every mistake in the book and, hopefully, learned from them. It was easy to be with him, that's for sure, a drama free zone. We both loved that.

Right from the get go Travis had told me that he didn't want to be married. That was okay with me. After having two bad marriages that were anything but drama free and then one wonderful marriage to Jake, I was done. When Jake tried to persuade me to find a new love after he was gone, I would always answer him that I would rather quit a winner. That's how I truly felt. Sure, I knew how great it could be, but I also knew how awful it could be. Who wants to be an old woman putting up with abuse or neglect? No thank you, I'm happy on my own.

One of the things on my bucket list was to ride in a horse and buggy through downtown Pittsburgh. It just always looked so romantic. I had asked Jake and a couple other suitors to do it, but, they always refused saying that the horses smelled too badly. Travis said sure right away. He was a farmer and owned a horse, he loved the smell.

I looked up the timing for the rides that started at Station Square, 8:00 to 10:00 every Friday and Saturday nights. We got dressed up so the photos would be nice and made the trip down. We waited at the horse stand, but the driver never showed up, we did this a couple of times. I was so disappointed and gave up on that idea.

But, one night in July, Travis decided to take me to dinner in Station Square. We came out of the parking garage and the horse and buggy was across the street. The driver was dressed in a tuxedo and top hat and the horse was simply beautiful, majestic. I started to run.

"Come on Travis, hurry! He's over there, let's get there before anyone else takes him. Hurry!" I ran across the street zigging and zagging through traffic. It was a wonder I didn't get hit. All I could think was to get over there before he rode off.

Travis came walking up behind me and inquired about a ride. I remember how distinguished the driver was.

"Why yes, my good man, please step right up. Here young lady take my arm and allow me to help you."

I was so excited, it was a dream come true. The night was so beautiful even in the city you could see so many stars shining. The driver rode us around and down through Bessemer Court to the river's edge. We could see the fountain at Point State Park and the place where the three rivers meet. The city lights reflected like diamonds on the water. It was so romantic.

You can understand my surprise when the driver stopped the buggy. Travis bounded out and then held out his hand to me to help me out of the buggy. I didn't know what to think, what was happening.

Then, just like that, Travis got down on one knee and proposed to me. I couldn't believe it. He had always said that he wasn't the marrying kind. For a moment, I was dumbstruck. It must have seemed an eternity to him as he awaited my answer.

When I finally collected myself, I said yes, of course I said yes. I loved this man more than anything. The whole night was just magical!

As soon as I said yes, Travis picked me up in his arms, kissed me and spun me around. We could hear the music coming out of the Hard Rock Cafe. Right there along the water's edge, Travis held me close and danced with me. The driver stood by smiling. It was like a fairy tale that I would never forget.

Chapter 51

Hi y'all, this is Travis. I found this manuscript amongst Tina's things. She didn't get to finish it, but, it sure feels like it deserves an ending. I was with her, you know, when it happened. It feels like I'm the likely candidate to tell the story. It sure was the strangest thing.

We had been dancing. She was so tiny and light on her feet, I loved to throw her around a bit. She always giggled and that just made me do it more. I remember the first time on the dance floor when I told her to jump to the left. She didn't know what was going to happen. But she did it, she always did trust me. She jumped up I caught her and spun her around, then I went down on one knee and landed her sitting on my other one. Her eyes were wide as saucers. She loved it.

That's where it happened, you know, on the dance floor. We sure loved to dance with each other. That was how we met, but then, I know she already told you about that. Of course, you didn't hear my side. It was love at first sight for me. I was really glad when she contacted me, I had a little too much baggage at the time to make the first move. She was wearing a bright red dress that showed off all her assets if you know what I mean. Oh yes, I noticed her as soon as she walked in with her friend. I knew she had never been there before, I would have remembered that one, yes, indeed. We were in a circle to learn the dance and I couldn't wait until it was my turn with her.

I spun her around and she giggled, I was hooked. You could just feel the joy of dancing radiate off of her. It felt to me like the joy of life itself. Her smile just lit up her whole face. It was hard to believe that she was new at dancing, she took to it right away. But then, I digress.

It makes me sad that we never got around to tying the knot. I should have asked her sooner, but, well, I didn't have much use for marriage, saw too many buddies of mine way too unhappy. You always think you have a lot of time – until you don't, right? Anyway, no use for regrets, just be happy for the time you had and the love you shared. What else can you do?

Did she tell you how I proposed? Oh heck, I'm just going to tell you again. One of the things on her bucket list was to ride in a horse and buggy. It seems she had asked a couple of guys to do it but they all said no, didn't like the smell of the horse. Me being a farmer and a prior owner of a horse, well the smell didn't bother me none, so I said sure.

You know we tried to catch up with that horse and buggy driver several times. He was supposed to be riding at Station Square every Friday and Saturday night in the summer. We went down and tried to find him but that little bugger always eluded us. Well, for the big event, I just couldn't take a chance. I called him up and made him promise me that he would be there at 8:00 that Saturday night in July. Tina thought we just got lucky. I got lucky alright.

We walked out of the parking garage and there he was. He did it right too. He was wearing a top hat and tuxedo and had the most beautiful white stallion hooked onto the buggy. He even brought a blanket in case she got cold.

We saw him and Tina took off running, dodging cars, with me close behind. It's a wonder we didn't get hit.

I gave him a wink when Tina wasn't looking.

"Hey, buddy, do you think the two of us can get a ride with you?"

"You are in luck, my good man, no one has secured my services."

I held her hand helping her step up into the buggy. She looked like dynamite in her skin tight black dress and silver high heels.

He drove us down along the river, the lights reflecting into it looked like colorful diamonds. Some music wafted off of Bessemer Court. Tina nestled into my shoulder. She just beamed with her dream coming true. Even the stars seemed to be cooperating to make it a magical night.

"I can't believe that we're in this horse and buggy, it's like a fairy tale for me. Thank you so much for agreeing to do this." She said giving me a big kiss.

The driver pulled over to the side. When we looked across the water, we could see the fountain at the point, lights glowing and the water bubbling up. This was the spot where the three rivers merged.

I hopped out of the buggy and took her hand in mine to help her down. She looked puzzled. I got down on one knee right there at the waterfront the sound of the trains racing by.

"Tina, you have to know that I am head over heels for you. I was hooked from the first day I met you. I can't think of a better life than going to bed each night with you in my arms and waking up to see those bright eyes each morning. Please do me the honor of becoming my wife. That would make me the happiest man in the world."

Tina looked down at me as tears filled her eyes and spilled down onto her cheeks.

"My dear man, I have waited so long to hear you say that. I have loved you from the first day I met you. I can't think of anything that would make me happier than to be your wife and spend my life with you. Yes, yes, of course I will marry you. You have made me so happy tonight!"

With that I jumped up and grabbed her in my arms and kissed her. To see her so happy filled my heart with joy.

So, that was a year ago. The happiest year of my life. Guess I got a little off track, but, it needed to be said.

We were back at the VFW for the swing dance that night. We would dance with other people but as soon as our eyes locked we would make our way back together. The DJ had just put on the great swing classic "In the Mood."

Tina ran across the dance floor and jumped into my arms. It was one of her favorite dance tunes. I spun her around mercilessly. She jumped to my left and I lifted her up, spun her and brought her around to my knee. We danced through the whole song with all of its false stops. She was laughing, full of joy.

When it was over, she hugged my neck, "Travis, let's go sit down for a moment. Come sit with me."

"Okay, sure darlin'." I took her hand.

Tina stopped walking and looked me right in the eyes with such tenderness.

"You know, Travis, I was right. I wouldn't have wanted to miss my time with you for anything in the world. You're incredible. I love you so much."

She left me speechless. I just picked her up in a warm embrace and kissed her lips, right there on the dance floor.

We walked over to the table her hand in mine and I gave her the bottle of water. She took a drink. As we sat down, she nestled into my shoulder and I could feel her heart racing. The quickness alarmed me.

"Tina, are you alright?"

She had a far off look in her eyes. That's when it happened, it was the darnedest thing.

She reached up with one arm, and got a sweet smile on her face.

"Oh you're here. Yes, yes, of course you can have the next dance."

I looked up to see who she was reaching for, talking to, but there wasn't anyone there.

"Who are you talking to, Tina?"

"Oh, it's Jake, Travis, Jake is here. He wants the next dance with me. It's okay, isn't it Travis, you don't mind, do you?"

I didn't know what to say. She took a deep breath, slumped back on to my chest and was gone. Her face looked like that of an angel.

And just that fast, my life became a lonely place.

The music played on. The dancers waltzed across the floor swirling to the music oblivious to the fact that over in the corner my heart was breaking.

I couldn't move.

I held her in my arms and gently kissed her head as a tear escaped my eye and slid silently down my cheek.

You know, she always joked about dying on the dance floor. She would always say, "What better way to go than doing what you love with someone you love, who loves you."

Tina always said that she was happy with her life. She was so proud of Sam and loved being his mother and she had two great loves in her life. Jake, of course, was the first and I'm proud to say that I was the second.

Well, I'll tell you what, Jake may be dancing with her now, but you better believe when I get there, I'm cutting in.

Made in the USA
Lexington, KY
13 January 2019